THE MASK OF CAIN

David P Garland

Dedicated to my mother, a true woman of faith.

CONTENTS

CHAPTER 1. PYRO

Howard had a nickname, donned in horror and jest when young, that stuck. It was "Pyro". He had a propensity for trying to burn things, especially the living.

He was a loner for sure. Nothing wrong with being a loner, but it was more than that. It was clear to most that Howard had psychopathic tendencies. From the first time Tripp met Howard, which was in the second grade, Tripp noticed that Howard avoided people, particularly those in authority. He had a mean streak. At first it didn't necessarily appear abnormal for an adolescent boy, but it wasn't something you would seek out either. He certainly was not the only bully in the school, but the mean streak progressed into a more destructive and malicious behavior over time, until people became scared of him. Not just the students, but the teachers and administrators of the school as well.

In the fourth grade, when Tripp was nine and Howard was in the same class but twelve, two police officers came to the math room in the morning and, after briefing the teacher by the entrance to the classroom in hushed tones, forcefully but courteously escorted Howard through the door and down the hall. The speculative mumbling didn't come close to anticipating what really led to his removal: stealing cigarettes (Howard smoked), beating up a 2nd grader, breaking a car window? No, we later found out that Howard was detained because someone's house had burned down early that morning, killing the elderly male resident and his dog as they slept. It was widely believed that Howard was the one that lit that house on fire, but it was never proven. He was questioned by the local police and let go that afternoon.

In addition to avoiding authority, Howard had no respect for it. And he clearly didn't place any value on human life either. It was well-known that his parents never disciplined him, and in fact seemed to encourage his reckless behavior. After they died, he was placed in a foster home that did its best to discipline him, but it was to no avail. When he stopped showing up for school, the school did very little to address the issue. The people around him felt threatened and were just as happy to see him go. In the end they felt there was nothing they could do for him anyway, and it was only a matter of time before he would be sent to juvenile detention or prison.

Eventually the foster home told him he wouldn't be able to stay there anymore. At that point he really had nowhere to go, except for his last living relative. So his grandmother, who was probably the kindest woman you'd ever want to meet, took him in. She was a church-going local saint, not at all what you'd expect from someone of that family. But she had very little contact with him growing up, as Howard's parents had pretty much cut her off from the family. She was well aware of his reputation, but lived by the principle that love can conquer all. She showered him with love in order to nurse him back to righteousness and character. It didn't go so well.

Howard was larger and older than all of his classmates, a function of being held back a grade more than once. But even for his age, he was quite large. He was also smart, brilliant as a matter of fact, but he just didn't seem to care and he never applied himself at school.

Apart from his size, there was nothing that stood out about his physical appearance, except for his eyes. Rarely would you have the opportunity to look into them as he was usually looking away from you or at the ground. But when he actually did look at you, you had an alarming sense that there was nothing there. It felt as though there was no presence behind them, like Howard was empty, dead or both. The first time Tripp had that experience a couple of years ago he immediately froze. Tripp forgot what he was going to say and stood in silence. Howard didn't blink and finally walked away.

Following Howard's removal from school, the only time Tripp saw him was at the 7-Eleven on Barrett Street, though he wouldn't say anything to him. Usually he'd be out front seated on the edge of the cement planter, "planted" with cigarette butts and crushed, empty soda cans, with a brown paper bag next to him. He was always holding a cigarette, often hunched over his legs, watching the ground or the never-ending progression of cars and customers entering and leaving the store.

One day, on a whim, Tripp decided that he would try to talk to him. He hadn't exchanged a word with him since the house-burning incident. He walked over to him as he stared at the ground with a cigarette in his hand. Tripp kept his distance but got close enough to speak to him without having to raise his voice across the parking lot. There was only one car parked in front of the store.

Howard's true mass didn't show when he was sitting. At twelve years old, he wasn't overweight, but he was dense and visibly strong. As Tripp approached, Howard continued to stare at the ground, unmoving. Tripp thought he hadn't even noticed him, but then he put his cigarette in his mouth, inhaled and looked up to exhale. His gaze was expressionless, the eyes had that same empty look they always had, and as the smoke slowly curled upwards in an unusually warm October breeze he locked Tripp with his gaze. After a few uncomfortable seconds Tripp looked down. Without saying a word Howard stood up from the planter, threw what remained of his cigarette on the ground and crushed it under the sole of his sneaker. A second car pulled into the lot and parked. The slammed car door and chime of the entrance to the store sounded in the distance. Tripp lifted his gaze from Howard's shoes, to his waist and finally his face. When their eyes met again Howard picked up the paper bag and simply said, "Follow me."

CHAPTER 2.
MR. TYLER

Tripp was a fairly simple kid growing up. Actually, let me rephrase that: his family and home life were complicated, and his thoughts were very tangled and inward-looking as a result; however, he kept the inner chaos at bay by making his outer life as prosaic as possible. Simple hobbies, simple routine. He did all the things that you would expect a normal boy growing up in lower middle-class suburbs to do.

As a family, his wasn't well-to-do by any stretch of the imagination, and he grew up with his parents and sister in a modest home in a modest neighborhood. Money was always tight and things were tense in the house. Not knowing any differently, he assumed the family dynamic was pretty much the norm.

His father had a drinking problem and would arrive home drunk pretty much every night, though the degree was variable. When less drunk he would pass out in bed usually without incident; when more drunk he would often pick a fight, which meant a tension-filled hour or longer between him and Tripp's mother. She would accuse him being a bad husband and father, of drinking away their every last penny in crappy bars, and of destroying the family. He would, in turn, accuse her of being an intolerable nag who didn't appreciate how hard he worked to pay the bills.

Sometimes household items would be thrown and broken, sometimes not, but more often than not the exchange would end with his mother falling asleep in her bedroom behind a slammed door, and his father passing out on the couch in the basement. Even though it was deeply unpleasant and caused crushing tension in mind and body for Tripp and his sister, he still assumed it wasn't outside the range of normalcy for a family.

Approximately once per week the fight between them would escalate further and there would be furniture and/or household items smashed, sometimes a hole forced into the living room wall, the sound of breaking glass and louder screaming. Tripp and his sister would wait tensely in bed, stiff as planks, listening anxiously for silence so they could fall asleep again. Sometimes on these weekly occasions they could hear them physically pushing and pulling each other. There were bruises and cuts, but fortunately no one ever seemed to get seriously hurt. On those particular nights they always feared the worst.

Apart from these altercations, there wasn't

a whole lot of excitement in Tripp's childhood home; at least until the events began, which will be covered in more detail later. His sister, four years younger than him, was the social, popular one. Apparently, he had a little brother born a year after his sister, but he never got to meet him. He was born prematurely and apparently died in the hospital the day he was born. His mother didn't get out of bed for weeks afterward and Tripp remembered being scared that she was dying too. He was only five at the time and didn't really understand what was going on. His parents never spoke about the loss and probably felt that if they never mentioned the incident it would be as if it never happened. Everything Tripp knew was from things they said to each other when arguing. Tripp never asked any questions.

When entering primary school Tripp wasn't self-conscious or shy and freely developed friendships with his classmates, occasionally got sent to the principal's office, held his own in recess kickball and did his homework. That changed as he grew older, and looking back he could almost pinpoint a shift to around this time when he lost a little brother. Things in the house seemed more tense from that point on. His mother never seemed to fully recover, his father's drinking really blossomed, and as a result Tripp became less social, less interested in friends, and started to prefer the security of books and fantasy. He began to see people as a risk and to reside more and more frequently in his thoughts, some real and many fabricated. The solitude and security of books and school came easily and naturally to him. He was both smart and intellectually curious, so this shift was comfortable, though at times lonely.

The change in family dynamic that occurred as a result of the loss of his brother wasn't the only event that sparked his journey inward, though he could see in retrospect that was when it started. It was more a confluence of events. First was the perpetual friction between his parents that seemed to grow much worse at that time. The sight of them doing battle and tearing each other down on a regular basis drove him inward. On top of that, Tripp was probably by nature a more introverted individual than an extroverted one. And third, a couple of years later, but probably the most substantive reason of the three, was his experience with his teacher Mr. Tyler. Those traumatic events definitely accelerated his transition from a social, well-adjusted boy to a progressively more self-absorbed and introverted one, walling himself off from the outside world.

Mr. Tyler was a teacher he trusted. He also happened to be Tripp's favorite teacher who taught his favorite subject in school: science. He looked forward to that class every day, until that trust was violated. A couple of months into the school year, Mr. Tyler asked Tripp to stay after class. He thought he was in trouble. He wasn't.

"Tripp, you're my best student. And I have

a special science project I would like to work with you on."

He was excited and relieved. He couldn't wait to find out what the project was.

"Wow, that's great Mr. Tyler. I would like that."

"We'll start next Wednesday after school if that works for you. I know you have Science Club that day, but I think this will be better for you. We can work at my house because this is a very secret project we'll be working on. I don't want any else at the school knowing about it."

Tripp could hardly contain himself. He felt really special that day and walked home dreaming thoughts of building a rocket ship or a time machine. Then he would tell himself how crazy that was and to grow up. Deep inside, Tripp did have a feeling that something was strange about the whole thing, but not enough to question anything at the time. He was more fixated on his curiosity and excitement about the project and for having been selected to work on it.

The impact of what ensued was profound and lasting. On the first day of their work together the following Wednesday, Tripp arrived at his science classroom shortly after 3:00 pm, after school had ended and most of the other students had already gone home on the buses. Mr. Tyler took him to his house, because Mr. Tyler said that the equipment for the experiment was located there, in a large toolshed behind his home. It's true that there was some science equipment in the shed, a workbench and some glass beakers, but there were more garden tools. The last thing he remembers from that day is that Mr. Tyler told him he needed to remove his clothes for the experiment, and that it was absolutely critical that he keep all of this to himself. The experiment had to remain a secret, and if he told anyone it would destroy the experiment forever and he would be in a lot of trouble. His body froze and his mind froze. He didn't want to disappoint his favorite teacher, or to get in trouble, and he simply went through the motions, this time and every time. Even years later, when Tripp thought about those incidents where Mr. Tyler molested him, his whole body would go numb and cold. It lasted for a few months, and they did do an experiment together actually having to do with science, but that was just a sideshow. Tripp didn't remember any details of the experiment. After a few months it stopped because Mr. Tyler was caught with another boy, Eric, a year younger than Tripp, and promptly disappeared from school. Tripp heard that Mr. Tyler had committed a serious crime and had gone to prison. But that's not actually the case.

Tripp didn't tell anyone, preferring to keep it a secret, more out of fear than anything else: he somehow thought he had done something wrong and he didn't want to get into trouble. He also wanted to forget those events, to bury them in the past, remove them from his memory forever. He couldn't say if there was any connection or not, but when he looked back on the experience he realized it was about that time that the visions began.

When the visions first started, Tripp didn't know what was happening. The first time he had one he thought that he had fallen asleep and was dreaming. It was a recurrence of the actual events with Mr. Tyler, but the events kept repeating, and each time seemed more real than the last. It also became hard to differentiate between dream and reality. He was lying in bed, and he was thinking about the last time he saw Mr. Tyler. They were painful images that he tried to erase, which only served to bring them into sharper focus.

He vividly remembered Mr. Tyler's blue dress shirt, the sleeves rolled up, his hair still blown out of position from the gusting wind outside. He was terribly uncomfortable and tense.

"Would you like something to drink? Maybe a juice?" He opened the refrigerator door and peered inside.

Tripp shook his head no.

"Ok. Well, I'm going to have one before we get started." Tripp felt his body twist tighter.

"You've been a good assistant, Tripp. We've been making good progress. But let's not forget our agreement...no one can ever know about our project. If anyone finds out, it will all be ruined."

Tripp nodded, shrinking further into the chair at the kitchen table.

Then a woman's voice filled the kitchen

from the living room. It was the voice of salvation.

"Honey, is that you? I finished early today!"

Tripp's relief at the sound of that voice was matched by Mr. Tyler's clear irritation. He put his drink down on the counter and stared at the door between the living room and the kitchen, forcibly veiling annoyance in his reply.

"Yes, honey, we're in the kitchen." By the time his wife entered, the tension was gone.

He asked her what brought her home so early.

"Well, there was a power outage in our office building. Actually, that whole section of town. Doesn't look like there's been any problem here though." She acknowledged Tripp seated at the table.

"Oh, hi, Tripp. Nice to see you again. How is the project coming along?"

"We're making good progress," Mr. Tyler quickly offered. "Tripp is a good assistant. Well, I guess I should be taking Tripp home now. Tripp, we'll definitely pick it up another time."

Tripp nodded in agreement. "Ok. Nice to see you Mrs. Tyler."

"Oh, honey, I have to run a couple of errands this evening. Is it ok if I use the car?"

"Sure," Mr. Tyler replied as they exited the kitchen. "I'm going to drop Tripp off at home and will be back in a little bit."

Tripp and Mr. Tyler made a swift exit and they drove to Tripp's house in silence. When they arrived, he pulled the car up to the curb and told Tripp he'd see him at school tomorrow. Tripp walked in the front door of his house, not knowing it would be the last time he'd see Mr. Tyler alive.

Tripp's visions began not too long after this incident, and that first recurring one was of this last trip to Mr. Tyler's house, suddenly ending with Mrs. Tyler entering the kitchen. Tripp couldn't say if they were dreams or visions, because he would see them sometimes when asleep, a dream, and sometimes when wide awake, a vision. In either case, the events seemed just as real as they did when they actually occurred.

It wasn't long after that when Mr. Tyler was arrested coming out of the school one afternoon. After Mr. Tyler's arrest, Tripp's mother mentioned it to Tripp when he got home from school.

She was standing at the kitchen sink and turned when he entered.

"Hi Tripp, I heard today that your science teacher was arrested today. Did you know that?"

He hesitantly replied: "Yes."

"I heard that he was acting inappropriately with some students at the school."

She turned to look at her son again, and after some time said, "Did he ever say or do anything to you Tripp? Did he ever hurt you in any way?" She looked pained to ask the question, and Tripp looked away, unsure how to respond.

"No." He was afraid it wasn't a very convincing response. He continued to look at the floor.

"Ok. Well, I hope you'd tell me right away if anything ever happened."

"I would."

And that was that. Tripp could tell by her expression that he hadn't put her entirely at ease, but that was the last they discussed it.

Tripp's mother didn't know that Mr. Tyler had selected him for an after-school project, because Tripp never brought it up, especially after the first visit to his home. Her understanding was that he was staying late for science club, so it never raised questions in her mind. He had found out the hard way that anything he revealed to one parent would often end up as ammunition in the heat of an argument between his parents, or be used against him instead. So he learned early on to keep things to himself. He remembered telling his mother one Sunday morning on the way home from church that he didn't understand how God could let so many bad things happen in the world if He loved us. So it was hard to believe He actually existed. She didn't respond at the time, but the next time Tripp's father came home drunk she blamed him for corrupting the children and turning them against God. And so on.

Over time he told her less and less. In fact, he found that he started to habitually lie to her, even when it was not of any benefit to do so, rather than tell her anything that might be used as a weapon.

C HAPTER 3.
SIGHTSEEING

"Where are you going?"

Tripp called the question out to Howard as he started walking away, but he wasn't going to answer. Howard headed around the side of the 7-Eleven, paper bag in hand, heading toward the parking lot in the back, and Tripp hesitantly started out in pursuit of him. He was walking at a moderate but deliberate pace, headed for the well-worn dirt path cutting across the lawn behind the store and into the woods. When Tripp saw that he was headed for the woods, he stopped, and reconsidered whether he should follow him, but he never looked back and his curiosity won over his trepidation. He kept on the path into the woods, which were quite large, but a common place for the children and teens of the town to play.

It was a beautiful fall afternoon, sunny with a warm breeze, but a breeze periodically laced with a sharp chill dusting the boughs and branches of the trees. The chill was enough to penetrate multiple layers of clothing. Howard trudged on, until they reached a spot with a large toppled tree where he sat down and pulled something out of the bag. As Tripp got a bit closer it appeared he had a bottle in his hand. He twisted off the top and took a drink. When Tripp sat down next to him he pulled a second identical bottle out of the bag and extended it toward Tripp with an invitation to try it. Tripp took the bottle from his hand asking what it was.

"It's juice. It's good. Try it."

The bottle was opaque so Tripp couldn't see the contents. There was no label either. But he was thirsty and if Howard was drinking the same thing he figured it was probably fine. Besides, he didn't want to appear scared, even if he was. Tripp screwed off the top and smelled the contents. It smelt good: sweet and savory, though he couldn't identify the smell. He took a sip and it tasted unusual but quite nice. He took another sip as Howard threw his empty bottle into the dead leaves, stood up and starting walking again. Tripp drank a bit more then continued a fair distance behind, but never losing sight of him, and thought better of drinking the whole bottle without knowing its contents. He put the top back on and threw it as far as he could into the woods, losing sight of it amongst the leaves on the ground.

Tripp wasn't sure how long it was, but after they walked a fair bit further he began to wonder whether he was actually heading any place in particular. That's when Howard stopped at the edge of a small dirt ridge. He was bent over it, looking onto whatever was on the other side. Tripp also stopped and watched him from a distance. He stood still for a while, then pulled another cigarette out of his pocket and lit it.

In spite of his interactions with Howard and having grown up in the same town with him, Tripp really did not know him at all or much about his background, and he'd had almost no interaction with him since the day he was kicked out of school. So most of what he knew about Howard came from what he'd heard from others, and Tripp knew that most of that wasn't very flattering. That said, Howard had never been anything but friendly to Tripp. A little strange, yes, but nothing like the rumors he'd heard about him. Quite frankly, Tripp found it hard to believe that Howard had done half the things he was accused of.

But as the walk through the woods dragged on, Tripp was beginning to wonder if he had made a mistake following him here, and whether he was actually in any danger. He continued to watch him from a distance, his view partially obscured by the trees. He smelt a whiff of smoke, as the wind wisped trails of Howard's cigarette in his direction. Tripp saw Howard take another drag then stomp it out under his foot, then he continued over the ridge and disappeared from sight.

Tripp continued onward and when he arrived at the ridge he spotted him a ways down the steep embankment following a lightly trodden, leafy trail at the bottom of the hill, running paral lel to the ridge. Tripp took a quick glance behind to see if anyone happened to be around, but the forest was empty. Tripp followed his lead and half-stumbled, half-ran down the embankment to the path he was on. After walking that path another 15 minutes or so he began to wonder whether he should head back. The October sun wouldn't be up much longer, and it seemed to be quickly getting darker already. He was also starting to get concerned if he would be able to find his way back because he had been following Howard, and not actually paying attention to any sort of landmarks to trace his path. He had been in the woods many times before, but the woods were expansive, and there were plenty of sections that he was not that familiar with, including this one. Tripp fell back a little further, seriously considering turning around when Howard took a sharp right behind a massive rock. He disappeared again and when Tripp turned the same corner he was just a few yards away looking into a large dirt hole which looked recently dug.

It was getting darker by the minute, the rays of the descending sun getting more and more filtered through the trees. Tripp walked up to his side and looked with him over the edge of the dirt pit in the ground. The image he was confronted with still haunts him to this day.

Sprawled face down in the dirt was what appeared to be a male body. It was clothed, and the clothes were ripped and bloody. The back of the head was bashed in and covered in a crusty, co-agulated mess of hair and blood. There were mag-gots swarming over the skin and areas where they had eaten away the flesh. Apparently, it had been there some time. Tripp caught a sudden whiff of the stench coming from the hole and it was over-powering. He buckled as he almost retched.

As the body was face-down, he couldn't tell who it was, but it was clearly a man: khakis and blue dress shirt, and no shoes. Tripp looked at Howard, horrified. He had never been to a funeral as a boy, never mind seen a battered corpse. Now the shadows and the sunlight were all melded to-gether in a growing darkness in the woods. He sud-denly became aware of the shock and fear pulsing through his body and blurted out a question:

"Howard, what is this?"

Howard didn't move. Neither did Tripp.

"Howard?"

Again, no response. He then stepped for-ward and jumped into the hole next to the body. He kicked the body over with his foot. Tripp gasped as he saw the dirty, bloody, but clearly defined face of Mr. Tyler who had an expression of horror frozen on his face. Tripp then recognized his all-too-fa-miliar uniform of khakis and a blue dress shirt.

"Oh my god. How did this happen, Howard? This is Mr. Tyler!"

"Yes."

"What is this?!"

Tripp had a sick, twisted knot in his stomach, a combination of dread, fear and repulsion. He was also somewhat numb as the body in front of him was that of the sick man who took advantage of him.

"How did this happen? Did you find him here?"

"I did it."

Part of Tripp knew right away that he was telling the truth. Part of him still couldn't believe, in spite of Howard's reputation, that he was capable of such a violent act. But here was flesh and blood evidence of it.

"I know what he did to you."

How in the world did he know that, Tripp wondered. He hadn't told anyone.

Howard continued. "He did it to others too. Not anymore." Tripp thought he detected a faint, one-sided smile on Howard.

Tripp knew exactly what he meant, but couldn't help but ask: "What are you talking about?"

"He had to pay. He can't do that to you."

Tripp was speechless. Apparently he anticipated Tripp's next question.

Howard simply said, "I just know things."

And that was all Tripp got.

Howard then picked up a shovel which was lying at the end of the ditch, and started shoveling the dirt from the mounds surrounding the grave, into it to cover the body. Tripp stood motionless and speechless as the body of Mr. Tyler began to disappear under the moist dirt.

Another stiff breeze blew the smell of rotting corpse into his nostrils and he fell on all fours. This time Tripp dry heaved for several minutes.

Suddenly overwhelmed with the shock of what he was witnessing Tripp simply said he had to leave, and left the way he came. He realized that it was now nearing dusk, and he began to walk faster, and then run. He wanted to get out of there as quickly as possible. He looked back periodically, through the growing shadows, to see if Howard was behind him. He wasn't, and in spite of his disorientation, he did manage to retrace his steps. He eventually saw the lights of the 7-Eleven through the trees where he had entered the forest. He followed the lights to the parking lot and walked home in the glow of twilight and streetlights.

The chaos of home was a welcome relief to the events of that afternoon. When he walked in the door his mother was cooking in the kitchen. She heard Tripp come in, and called to him. As soon as she saw Tripp she asked what was wrong.

"Nothing."

"Tripp, don't lie to me. I can tell something's wrong. What did you do?"

Tripp hadn't noticed his sister until she looked up from her homework at the kitchen table.

"No, really, nothing. I just saw that guy Howard at the store. He scares me."

Tripp wanted out of there and hoped that would be enough to satisfy her. He started to leave but she continued her investigation.

"Tripp. What did I tell you about that boy Howard?"

"Really Mom, I didn't do anything. I just saw him but that was it. I didn't even talk to him."

He glanced at his mother. She clearly didn't know what to think.

"I need to do my homework." And he left.

The image of Mr. Tyler, dead, mangled, in a ditch, covered in blood, would not leave, and the more he tried to forget the incident, the more it consumed him.

How could Howard live with the knowledge that he took another man's life? Had he really burned down that house, killing the man inside? How many lives had he taken? Part of him felt as though he should tell someone, but a bigger part of him wanted to not have anything to do with it, which meant trying to forget about it altogether. Who would he tell anyway? He made a decision to try to put it behind him, with very little success.

And that was the night, lying in bed, that the visions began. As mentioned previously, the first vision was his last interaction with Mr. Tyler at his house, his wife's interruption, and as quickly as it started, it ended and he was back in his bedroom.

He had that vision a few times, which was about events that had actually occurred. Then a few weeks later he had a new vision, also related to Mr. Tyler, but this time it was about things that had never happened.

In this one he clearly saw Mr. Tyler open the front door of his house to find two policemen on his doorstep. Both policemen were in full uniform and polite but firm. They told Mr. Tyler that he had to come with them. Those were the only words that were audible. They continued to carry on a conversation, but there were no audible words coming out. He then got into the police car and they drove off. It was night, and the sky was pitch black. No moon, no stars.

Then Tripp saw a swarm of black vultures swoop in to the front yard. They landed and started pecking at raw flesh now littering the ground, pecking at flesh on bone, hundreds of them. They kept coming, covering every inch of the yard.

There was a stench of rotting flesh everywhere, the same vile smell as in the woods, and a blood red full moon rose above the horizon. Then in a violent rush of wind it was all gone and he was abruptly back in his bedroom. Similar to the other vision, this one kept recurring and would always end at the same point of the rising moon.

With each of these visions, the first time it was clear to Tripp he was seeing things. But as they recurred, every time it became harder to distinguish. He would tell himself it was not real, but he experienced it as all too real. Sometimes he became confused during and after the episodes, and it would take progressively longer to convince himself that he was actually back in reality. At one point he started to get scared that he might lose his ability to distinguish between the two altogether.

The third vision of these early episodes was the strangest of them all. It started with Tripp in school, looking out the classroom window. The schoolyard was completely swarmed with black vultures again, this time larger than before, and pecking at corpses. In their midst, in the middle of the courtyard was a fruit tree, but they kept their distance from it. The circumference of the tree was clear of the birds and the bodies. The tree was completely covered with the large, heavy fruit, yet not weighed down. It was not a fruit Tripp had seen before, like some sort of mix between a grapefruit and an apple.

Then the fruit started dropping off the tree, one by one, and as it fell to the ground, the vultures would venture under the tree close enough to grab the fallen fruit in their beaks and then fly off. One by one they fell, and one by one they were taken by the birds out of sight, until both the tree and the field were barren. At that point the tree withered and died, the sky went black, and someone grabbed Tripp from behind though he didn't see his face. He woke up with a start.

All of these visions occurred on multiple occasions, sometimes while he was asleep, but not always. Sometimes he would have them at random times throughout the day. It didn't seem to follow any pattern or to be triggered by any particular event. When they occurred during the day, he tried to ignore them and stay focused on where he was in the moment, but he couldn't stay out of them for very long. Eventually they would consume his attention and he would be drawn in again until the episode ended.

There were other visions as well, some recurring over long periods of time, others just a few times. They weren't all as memorable; many were much more mundane. There were also periods when they would stop. Tripp often thought that perhaps they were over for good, but then they would suddenly start again, even more vivid than before. Fact is, even with intermittent breaks, they were now a permanent feature of Tripp's life and would never end.

C HAPTER 4. AWAKENING

Tripp knew that Howard was trouble, but as mentioned before, he never used to believe the worst allegations that swirled around town regarding him. Now he knew he was fully capable of anything. In a strange way, he was grateful for Howard looking out for him. He had felt completely trapped and incapable of protecting himself in the situation with Mr. Tyler. Yet, the scene he witnessed in the woods would be with him forever. Had Howard actually killed him? Tripp used to think that Howard was just mad, with a lot of pent-up anger inside. But now he knew that Howard was violent and dangerous. He never saw him with a look of anger on his face. In fact, he couldn't recall ever seeing any expression on his face. Howard seemed to always be without any affect at all. What made him turn out like that? Surely, he wasn't born that way. But whatever it is in the human psyche that enables feelings of remorse, joy, anger or sadness, Howard didn't seem to have it.

Tripp didn't see Howard again for some

time. In fact, he was probably avoiding the 7-Eleven out of fear of seeing him, but a couple of months after the incident in the woods he was passing by the store on his way to basketball practice and there he was. He was sitting in his usual spot on the planter, huddled up in a winter coat, smoking a cigarette. Tripp stopped short. Howard didn't acknowledge him, even when he stood directly in front of him on the street. He made a beeline for the entrance, still not even a glance. He purchased a Coke and left the store, but was surprised to find him no longer there. Curious, he scanned the street in front of the store and the parking lots on either side, but no sight of him. He wondered if he wasn't imagining things as he continued on his way to practice. As much as he tried not to let it affect him, seeing Howard again rekindled all the anxiety and fears he had successfully avoided dealing with for many weeks. They were very present once again, and he was anxious all the way to the school gym. At practice he was clearly preoccupied, and when he missed his third shot of the night during the practice game the coach asked him where his head was and benched him.

When practice finished Tripp started home on his own, still wondering where Howard had gone. In the dark, frigid night he became anxious that perhaps he was hiding somewhere, waiting for him. He began to walk faster, then run, until he was out of breath, then continued walking quickly.

Ever since the incident in the woods he had begun locking his bedroom door at night, and now that the weather had turned colder he made sure his windows were securely locked as well. But he wondered if that was enough. A few blocks from his house he was jolted out of his anxious thoughts by the honking of a car horn behind him. He jumped and turned to see his father's car. He rolled down the window and called him.

"Hey Tripp. Hop in." He was in an unusually good mood and didn't appear drunk for a change. That was confirmed when Tripp didn't smell any alcohol after climbing into the car.

"Hi Dad. How come you're coming home so early?" If his father came home at all, it was usually long after Tripp was asleep, especially on a Friday.

"Tripp, you're looking at a new man."

He looked at him quizzically.

"Yes, son. All of our troubles are over now. I can't wait to tell your mother. Everything is going to be different from now on!"

Tripp's thoughts were all over the place and he remained speechless. What he was saying didn't really register.

"That's great Dad. How is that?"

"Well, Tripp, I gave up the drinking. I don't need to drink anymore. Things are going to be different," he repeated as he beamed.

"Great Dad."

Tripp had heard his father promise that he

was done with drinking countless times before, but it didn't seem to last very long. This time he seemed much more convinced though. Tripp really did hope this time was different.

He didn't say anything else during the drive of the remaining few blocks. He pulled up in front of the garage door. No sooner did he turn the car off than Tripp's mother came out of the house hysterically screaming as she ran toward the car door.

"Sarah's gone!" she shrieked. "She's gone. There's blood." She gasped for breath.

Tripp's father jumped out with the car still running and grabbed one of her flailing arms. It probably didn't register in her current state that he wasn't drunk, and was home early, both of which were highly unusual.

"What happened? Tell me what happened?" He was starting to take on some of her panic.

"Sarah's gone. And there's...there's blood! On the rug. I came home and the door was...open. The door was open and I can't find her anywhere." She struggled to catch her breath again, and Tripp felt the panic himself as he got out of the car. Tripp's father ran into the house and his mother followed, the screen door slamming behind her. Tripp followed them inside, but his mother pounced on him as he opened the front screen door.

"Tripp, you stay out of here! I don't want you in here!"

All he could see were blood stains on the living room floor and couch. It also looked like a trail of blood coming down the stairs. There was a broken lamp on the floor.

Tripp's father echoed her. "Tripp, you heard your mother. Go wait in the car."

Tripp reluctantly complied and returned to the passenger seat of the car, anxiously watching the screen door. The car was still running, as well as the heater, and he adjusted the vent so the warm air blew on him directly. He wondered what happened to his sister Sarah. Was she hurt, kidnapped, murdered? By whom? Who could possibly want to hurt her? It didn't make sense. As far as Tripp knew, everybody liked Sarah. Could it have been Howard?

These thoughts were racing through his mind when his father came out the front door. He realized that there were now two police cars parked in front of the house. He hadn't noticed their arrival. His father walked over to the cars to greet the three officers, and the four of them entered the house. Tripp heard another car pull up and turned to see a third police car arrive and two more officers get out and enter the house. Tripp also noticed some neighbors beginning to collect on the sidewalk across the street to observe the activity and make comments amongst themselves.

Tripp continued to wait and watch, fidgeting with the handle for the car window, opening it and closing it, ad infinitum. He turned to look behind himself again. Another officer was now interacting with the crowd, which had continued to grow larger. Two of the original officers came out the front door and returned to one of the police cars. Between basketball practice and the chaos at home, at this point Tripp felt completely drained. He resigned himself to stay out of the fray, and reclined the seat to close his eyes, while awaiting further directions from his father. Tripp quickly dozed off, and there he saw Sarah.

***

Sarah looked much older, more mature, but still clearly Sarah. She looked older than Tripp at this point, probably nineteen or twenty. She was walking down the street in a large city, in the evening. She seemed happy and walking with purpose. She turned the corner by a small grocery store, and met a young man there, in a suit. They kissed on the lips, then he led her around the side of a black car and opened the door for her. After she climbed in, he shut the door and Tripp could see the door lock. Something wasn't right. He didn't get in the car but stood outside. She tried to open the door but couldn't unlock it. Suddenly there was a massive tree busting through the cement street under the car, piercing straight through and emerging through the car roof. Continuing to grow, the top of the tree disappeared from sight into the dusky sky. The lower boughs of the tree bore the strange fruit Tripp had seen in other visions. The tree was massive and the fruit began to grow and ripen in fast-motion, finally falling off the branches under its own weight. The fruit was large and dense,

THE MASK OF CAIN

heavy enough to put deep dents in the car as it fell on the hood and roof. Then more and more fruit began to ripen and fall, rapidly crushing the car and burying it under its weight. Sarah was still inside screaming, banging on the car door and window, but she was trapped and the man didn't budge. Eventually the car was completely buried, but he could still hear his sister screaming and banging on the window.

***

The banging on the window startled Tripp awake, and he opened his eyes to see his mother rapping on the window and calling him to wake him up. He was still in a panic from the dream about his sister and as he opened the door for his mother.

"Tripp, come inside. The police need to speak with you for a minute."

He turned the car engine off and got out of the car. After taking another moment to get reoriented, he followed his mother into the house.

"It's ok Tripp. The policeman just wants to ask you a couple of questions. He's in the kitchen."

Tripp walked into the kitchen and sat down at the table where two officers were already seated and invited Tripp to join them.

"Hi, Tripp. I'm Officer Harrison, and this is Officer Pinter." They sat on either side of Tripp at the ends of the table.

"I know this is probably a confusing time for you, but we just want to ask you a few questions to help us figure out what happened here today. We're going to do everything we can to find your sister Sarah."

Tripp nodded that he understood.

"Tripp, when was the last time you saw your sister?"

He tried to recall and thought it was the day before. He didn't remember seeing her at all that day. He looked at the other officer, Pinter, then back at Harrison.

"Do you remember when that was?"

"Last night. At dinner."

"Ok. Good. Thank you, Tripp. At dinner, did you notice her acting strangely in any way? Did she seem nervous or upset?"

Again, he thought about it. He wasn't really paying much attention to anyone at dinner, especially his sister. He was probably thinking about his own stuff, though what exactly, he couldn't recall. The only thing he did remember was her getting scolded by their mother for feeding the dog from the table.

"I didn't notice anything last night. She seemed the same as she always does."

"Ok. Do you remember her sharing anything or talking about anyone new she's met recently at school or after school?

Again, nothing.

"Ok, Tripp, great. Final question: is there anyone you're aware of that would want to hurt her in any way?"

That question bothered Tripp.

"No, no! Of course not! There's no one. I don't think there's anyone who would want to hurt her. Everyone likes Sarah."

The officer stood up, looked over at his mother whom Tripp noticed was now standing by the kitchen door, then looked back at Tripp, who was clearly distraught.

"Ok, Tripp. That's fine. You've done a great job. Really helped us out a lot here.
We don't have any more questions for you right now."

Tripp waited to see what was next. His parents walked the officers out of the house, and he sat in silence, with only the clicking of the second-hand from the wall clock over the kitchen sink and muffled voices from the front of the house to occupy his mind. He got up and entered the living room. His parents were still speaking with the last two officers on the front lawn. The rest of the policemen climbed into their cars and left.

The saw the blood stains again on the carpet. He had no idea if they were Sarah's or not and he avoided them as he made his way to the couch. He also noticed, for the first time, that one of the end tables was knocked over where the brown ceramic lamp lay broken on the floor. The discussion on the lawn then came to an end and the last two officers left.

Tripp was sitting on the couch when his mother came back into the house, went upstairs and shut the bedroom door. She didn't say a word, and Tripp wondered what this meant. His father remained outside for a bit longer, then Tripp watched as he got into the car and drove away. He lay down on the couch and stared at the ceiling. Once again, after some time he began to descend into another fitful, yet vivid vision.

***

Sarah was sitting in a full school auditorium, their middle school, which she hadn't begun yet, but again she was older. She was staring at the stage, which was empty. Tripp couldn't fully see her face from the back corner. Everyone was looking at the stage, presumably waiting for something to start. The auditorium was full of folding chairs, and every seat was occupied. It appeared that they were all students, all about the same age, at least from behind. There was one door, locked shut with a chain and padlock, and covered in thick vines. It looked like others had tried to break through the vines to reach the door to escape, but they were all ensnared and at varying levels of rotting decay. Then Tripp realized that there was no presentation, and that everyone in the room was a corpse, including his sister. He walked toward the corpses, and caught a glimpse of the rear row. Their mouths were open and full of rotten food, which in some cases had fallen out of their mouths and onto their laps. There was no movement amongst any of them. Then, as he looked at them one by one they would disintegrate and vaporize into dust until there were no bodies left in the auditorium except that of his sister. Tripp tried to get to Sarah before she disappeared as well, but it was too late.

***

Tripp heard a bang and he opened his eyes. His mother had slammed the front door shut and muttered something about his father before walking into the kitchen.

Tripp stared at the kitchen door for a moment then closed his eyes again, what he saw in the auditorium still very fresh in his mind. He couldn't get the terrifying image of his disappearing sister to go away. He felt her, he felt her terror at whatever she and the rest of the room saw before they were frozen in death. He reopened his eyes and looked out the window at the darkness which now consumed the living room. The sound of a car driving past the house could be heard. Still trying to make sense of it all, he sat in silence, his mind drifting back and forth between the events of the evening and what he saw in the vision. He wondered if there was any connection. He watched shadows dance on the living room walls and ceiling as the wind swayed the shadows of tree branches in the streetlights and the moonlight. From time to time the sound of another passing car broke the stillness. After being lost in his thoughts for some time he finally came back to his senses and made his way into the kitchen. His mother wasn't there, but he spotted her sitting on the back porch.

He opened the door to the basement to see if his father had returned. Often when he came home he would come in through the basement entrance to avoid a confrontation, and watch television there until he sobered up or things cooled off. There was a dim light on but no sound. When he was there the television would always be on, even when he was sleeping. The background noise presumably helped him fall asleep. Tripp descended halfway down the stairs and knelt to peer into the finished room at the couch where his father usually slept since his mother told him he couldn't sleep in their bed anymore. That had happened during one of their more intense, drunken fights a couple of months before. The nightlight next to the sofa was what gave the room its glow. He returned to the kitchen to find himself something to eat. Given everything going on he knew that there wouldn't be any dinner that evening. After some successful foraging he went upstairs to his bedroom to read a bit and eventually fell into a dreamless sleep, where he stayed through the night.

The next morning, when he awoke, he went downstairs to find his mother on the telephone in the kitchen while sipping coffee. It was early. His father wasn't around. She didn't acknowledge Tripp as he entered the room and continued her conversation. Tripp grabbed one of the overused Tupperware bowls and poured himself some cereal.

"No, nothing."

"Uh, huh. Ok."

She finally looked at Tripp as though she wanted him to provide an answer. He assumed she was trying to find out any information she could about his sister.

"Ok. Thank you."

She hung up the phone, clearly dissatisfied. It was a Saturday, so they didn't need to prepare for work or school.

Tripp got the milk out of the fridge and poured some on his overfilled bowl. "Mom?"

No response. He ate a couple of spoonfuls. "Mom?"

She finally looked up. "Yes, Tripp. What is it?"

"Did they find out anything about Sarah yet?"

"Not yet Tripp. We still don't know anything."

Tripp's mother left the kitchen and he finished the rest of his breakfast in silence. He checked the basement again to see if his father has stumbled back at some point during the night. He hadn't, which wasn't unexpected. After washing his bowl he grabbed his coat, left the house and just started walking, no particular destination in mind. Tripp felt a need to move. It was a beautiful, sunny, warm day, quite unusual for December. After meandering aimlessly a few blocks he decided to walk to the part of the woods where he

had last been with Howard a couple of months before. He wondered if Mr. Tyler's body would still be
lying in the same place. Surely it was covered over
by Howard and all the fallen autumn leaves. The
woods were large, but he was pretty sure he could
retrace his steps to the site and locate the body. He
started in that direction.

The streets to the woods were quiet for a
Saturday morning. The 7-Eleven had no customers
inside as he passed around it and followed the path
into the woods. He retraced his steps from the last
time and had no problem finding the break from
the path that led to where he had seen Mr. Tyler
lying not that long before. The journey seemed a
lot faster this time. On arriving at what he believed
was the makeshift grave, he saw uneven ground
where dirt had been removed and then returned
to its original spot, albeit unevenly. He stood looking over the ridge, but then began to wonder if
he was in the right spot. There were several areas
all around him that he could see had similar uneven terrain. They were all covered by dead, brown
leaves that had fallen weeks before. The trees
didn't seem quite like he remembered them at the
grave site either. He kicked some of the leaves
up to see the ground underneath, but the ground
didn't look like it had been dug up in the recent
past. There were no familiar markers that he could
identify to confirm he was in the right spot. Apart
from where he had kicked up leaves, the ground
didn't look like it had been disturbed in months.

In fact, the clearing looked as though it had never been touched. He walked over to another section of the woods that looked like another good candidate for the scene of the incident. Same result. He saw one more, a little further in. Same thing with this one as well. He sat on a fallen tree trunk and looked up through the tops of the trees at the direction of the sun. The sunlight shone at a steep angle through the branches of the largely barren trees. He felt a bit of a warm breeze waft through the woods and stir some placid leaves as it progressed across the ground.

Tripp laid down on the forest carpet and continued to stare upwards. It was one of those moments of still, solitary peace that we take with us when we need it in a future tempest. He wasn't sure how long he was there, but he felt he would be perfectly content to lie there forever. In his tranquility, however, he was suddenly jolted. He faintly smelled cigarette smoke which caused him to bolt upright and look around for the source. He was shocked to find Howard sitting just a short distance away. He was sitting on a rock watching Tripp as he took a big inhale.

Tripp was irritated. There was something deeply wrong and unsettling in his presence. But Tripp was also starting to feel a vague sense of being inextricably tied to him, as if somehow their lives were starting to sync up via some strange cosmic force.

"How long have you been here, Howard?"

"Dunno."

"Did you follow me here?"

"No."

Tripp pushed up off the ground and stood up, brushing the leaves off that were stuck to his pants and coat.

Pointing just behind the ridge, he asked, "What happened to Mr. Tyler's body?"

"Mr. Tyler wasn't here."

"Come on Howard! You know you brought me here to see him."

Tripp was unusually short-tempered that morning, and Howard's cryptic responses were enough to tip him over.

"Howard, really! I'm not kidding. Where is Mr. Tyler? What happened to the body that was here? Did you bury it? I was with you, we saw it, and I will never forget it! Where was it if it wasn't here? I can't tell if this is the same location you took us to last time."

He took another inhale, then extinguished the cigarette on the side of the rock he was sitting on.

"It's not."

"Ok, fine, Howard. Where was it then? I know it was close to here."

"I don't remember exactly. He's gone now. No need to bother his spirit. It's gone now. Let it stay that way."

"What are you talking about?!" Tripp really didn't want to decipher Howard's cryptic language. He just wanted a straight answer. He wanted to find the location that had led him to panic not many weeks before, thinking that perhaps this would help him to put the whole thing to rest. Or was that really it? How would going back there put anything to rest? Tripp realized he wasn't sure why he felt compelled to return to the site.

"Howard! What do you mean?"

"I mean what I said. He's gone and I don't want him drawn back."

Tripp had no idea what Howard was trying to say, and that was as far as he was willing to pursue the subject. All the sudden he felt a pain in the back of his neck, then he started to feel a little unsteady and lightheaded. He bent over to get the blood flowing to his head again.

Howard took note of Tripp's discomfort but didn't react.

"Howard, I'm going to tell what happened!" Tripp thought a threat might get Howard to be more cooperative. Again, no visible reaction.

With that, Tripp resolutely turned and started walking back the way he had come. Howard was crazy and dangerous, Tripp kept telling himself.

"I never want to see him again."

Tripp realized he had spoken those last words out loud. He repeated that mantra over and over to himself and rode that conviction all the way home.

He was relieved to find the familiar face of his mother in the living room when he arrived back home. She was calmly sitting on the couch watching television. She smiled when she saw him enter.

"Tripp, where have you been?" Then his sister entered the room from the kitchen!

"...I told you we had ice cream, Mom. Oh, hi, Tripp."

She sat down on the couch next to her mother and began to eat ice cream straight out of the carton.

"Shut the door Tripp, it's chilly outside."

Tripp was in shock. "When did you get home?" he asked his sister, dumbfounded.

"A little while ago. I was at Jeanie's."

It was a perfectly logical explanation.

"Mom, what happened?"

"Your sister was fine Tripp. She knows better than to do that again though or she'll get a whipping she'll never forget. And she's grounded."

"Ok, Mom!"

"You are absolutely grounded, and you will buy us a new lamp young lady! Plus, you have to finish cleaning the carpet. Your sister, it turns out, was playing games in here with her friends who were definitely not supposed to be here." She was trying to suppress her happiness that her daughter was ok, by feigning anger.

"But where did you go Sarah?"

"I told you! I stayed at Jeanie's last night."

"I can't believe you did that and didn't tell Mom. We thought you were kidnapped or something! You left the living room a mess."

Sarah laughed loud and long, clearly not getting how scared the rest of the family had been. "Yes, I told Mom I was sorry. Tricia got a big cut, and we got scared and ran to her house. Her Mom's a nurse."

"Tripp, what's wrong with you?" Tripp had dealt with enough confusion, stress and drama to last him for quite some time. Somehow he felt like he had switched roles, that he was no longer the son but the worried parent, and that his mother wasn't as upset as she should be. He changed the subject, but the one he landed on didn't help.

"Where's Dad?"

"Your father is gone as he always is...never home when his family needs him."

Tripp realized his mistake as soon as he said it, and he let it go at that. He noticed the pressure building up in the back of his head and neck again. He was, of course, glad that his sister Sarah was safe and sound, but he also didn't like being needlessly terrified that his sister was...well, whatever he had spent the night and morning fearing. He noticed that the broken lamp had been cleaned up and it appeared as though the blood stains had been largely scrubbed out of the carpet. And that was that.

C HAPTER 5.
PASTOR TOM

Tom Polte was a large, exceptionally friendly and outgoing man who headed Tripp's family church. Tripp didn't know how long he had been the pastor there, but he knew it had to have been a while, because he had heard that Tom Polte became a pastor during a war, and had been at this church ever since. Tripp didn't know which war, but it seemed to him that the war being referenced was a long, forgotten one, and therefore Pastor Polte, or Pastor Tom as most people addressed him, had been there for quite some time.

Tripp liked him. In some ways he felt like Tom was more of a father to him than his own father was. His father was not around much; Pastor Tom was always there. His father would get drunk or angry for seemingly no reason; Tripp couldn't recall ever seeing Pastor Tom get mad, never mind drunk. Pastor Tom liked to ask Tripp questions, and spend time with him. His father spent most of his free time at bars, or sleeping on the couch, or arguing with his mother. So it was an easy choice to spend time with Pastor Tom rather than stay at home.

Pastor Tom knew Tripp's father from a few brief meetings with him, usually with Tripp's mother in tow for protection. Church was his mother's way of bringing stability into a chaotic home. His mother felt a duty to attend, and to make sure her children attended as well. Tripp's father, on the other hand, really had no interest in setting foot inside of their church, or any church for that matter.

His father was, to a large extent, an unsettling presence in Tripp's life growing up, and perhaps as a result he was untrusting of the people around him. Perhaps not. But the theory seemed reasonable. This distrust started at a young age. His experience with Mr. Tyler eradicated the possibility of that changing anytime soon.

After that incident he didn't try to trust people, he just kept to himself. Except with Pastor Tom. For some reason Pastor Tom was an exception. Looking back on it, Tripp wondered if perhaps he wasn't the same way, in spite of his gregarious personality, when he was a boy. They understood each other. Tripp's mother once told him that Tom had lost his first wife in a horrific car accident, and that Pastor Tom never fully recovered from that event. He had been driving on a country road one sunny, winter afternoon when a large animal of some sort jumped out in front his car and he abruptly swerved to avoid hitting it. The skidding car slammed into a telephone pole, and the pole snapped, crushing the passenger side of the car. His wife was instantly killed, while he sat in the driver's seat next to her with some serious cuts and scrapes, but otherwise unscathed. Tripp couldn't imagine witnessing an event like that and then having to go on with life with those images seared into memory forever.

After a lengthy period of mourning Pastor Tom returned to the pulpit one week as if he had just returned from a long vacation. No vestige of the traumatic scars visible, he resumed his normal life as the same kind, generous, loving man he had always been. But those who knew him well recognized a subtle, yet persistent sadness in his eyes and face that never left him. Tripp never detected it, but he also never knew him before the accident either. Pastor Tom never brought up the subject of his late wife. Tripp only knew about it from his mother.

Pastor Tom lived a modest life, in a modest house, eventually sharing it with a modest second wife. The second marriage took place not too long after he returned that day to preach. She was also a widow, a member of his church, and a perpetually joyful servant.

One day, after school, Tripp went to visit Pastor Tom at the church and his wife, Bess as everyone called her, greeted him at the door to the church office.

"Hi there Tripp!" she sang. "Tom's been looking forward to seeing you!"

Tripp smiled as he entered the building. He'd been looking forward to seeing him as well.

He waited in the lobby to his office as he usually did, while she went to get him. He could hear the singing voices of choir practice coming from the sanctuary. Pastor Tom soon came out to greet him and seated Tripp in his office while he went to take care of something with his wife.

Tripp scanned the contents of his office, as he had many times before, while seated on the couch by the door. His eyes landed on one of the photos on the wall which he didn't remember seeing before. There were a lot of them from his many travels around the world, most of them from when he was much younger, though some more recent. The one that caught his attention was a picture of Pastor Tom holding an object with a purplish color to it. From his position, Tripp couldn't make out what it was so he walked over to have a closer look. In the photo he was by himself, and the object appeared to be a piece of fruit, but what caught Tripp's attention in particular was the shape and color of the fruit itself. It looked vaguely familiar. Not something that he had eaten before. Then it struck him. It looked like the fruit from the dreams he had had on multiple occasions. It was a bit smaller than those in his dreams, but of the same shape and color. He could only describe it as looking like a mix between a grapefruit and an apple, but the color of a light plum. He looked at the surroundings in the photo, but couldn't tell where he was. Though the picture was a bit sun-faded, the landscape looked incredibly lush and green. There were vines and flowers of just about every color imaginable in the background. A much younger Pastor Tom was wearing short sleeves and a hat in the photo, and he had a stern look on his face while he held the fruit up to the camera. There was no one else in the photo.

"So, how you been Tripp?" Pastor Tom startled him as he reentered the room. He sat behind his desk, covered with all kinds of papers, books, t-shirts and memorabilia from trips and family and who knew what else. The desk was pretty disheveled.

"See something interesting in the pictures?"

Tripp felt a little like he had been caught peeking at something private. "Yeah, I saw this photo here with this thing that looks like a piece of fruit."

"Ah yes, there are some great photos up there, aren't there?"

"Yes, you traveled a lot."

"Well, I love to travel. But I don't travel nearly as much as I used to these days. I miss it."

"So, this photo. I don't remember seeing it before. Where is it from?"

"Hmmm." He looked out the window for a moment. "Good eye Tripp. That's a very interesting photo, that one." Another pause. Tripp's curiosity was building.

"That was taken in the Middle East. I was there many, many years ago. Unfortunately, you can't get to that place anymore."

Tripp looked at the photo again. "Where in the Middle East? And why can't you go there anymore?"

"Well, it's actually a spot in what's now Iraq. But it's very hard to find and now it's been lost."

"Lost?"

"Yep, lost. Or at least that's what they say. Many years ago, they shut down the area, and then after that, even though several have tried, no one has been able to locate that spot anymore. I tried to get permission to join a group of historians and scientists that was going to identify that location, but they ended up canceling our visas and our trip. A number of others who have attempted to find it haven't had any success. It's a bit of a mystery."

Tripp was fascinated. "It must be a special place."

"About as special as they come. Someday I'll tell you more about it. But enough about that. Tell me how you're doing?"

Tripp moved to the chair in front of his desk and sat down. He was still on the subject of the photo. "It's weird because I had a dream, in fact I've had the same dream several times. And I think I saw that fruit in it. I don't think I've ever seen it before, except in the dream, and now in your photo. They look almost exactly the same."

Pastor Tom's expression quickly changed.

Tripp wasn't sure why and he didn't explain. "That's interesting Tripp. But perhaps it's just because you've seen that picture before. It's been there forever."

Tripp realized that perhaps he was right. He didn't remember seeing it before, but it is true that he had been in that office countless times before. It probably did get in his head somehow even if he didn't notice it.

Pastor Tom tried to change the subject again.

"I heard you had a lot of things going on at home, some of them not so pleasant."

Tripp wasn't sure what he was referring to. It was probably just Sarah being stupid and going to her friend's house without telling anyone.

"I mean, as a smart young man like yourself, life can be a bit confusing even when everything seems normal on the outside."

"Did Mom tell you something?"

"Well, your mom did say she was concerned about you and that maybe you're struggling with some things."

Tripp had no idea what his mother could have said, and his face reflected this fact.

"She probably just wanted me to make sure everything was ok with you. How's school going for you lately?"

"Ok. I like it ok."

"That's good to hear. Have you been having any trouble with the other boys at school?"

Tripp thought of Howard, but he wasn't really a schoolmate. At least not anymore. Apart from that, he didn't interact much with the other students. The thought of Mr. Tyler came up again, which made Tripp start to feel very uncomfortable and guilty, so he quickly pushed it out of his mind.

"No, not really."

"That's great to hear, Tripp. I mean, I remember back when I was in school, I used to get picked on by some of the older kids. They made fun of me because I was a bit of a nerd, and definitely not any good at sports. Kids can be mean sometimes, for no good reason. Until they grow older that is."

He smiled and added, "And sometimes, even when they grow older they don't grow up." Pastor Tom chuckled at himself and Tripp smiled back.

"Tripp, tell me about your friend Howard."

Tripp now knew what he was trying to get at. But that was not a question he had anticipated. He tensed up a bit and tilted his chair backwards.

"When was the last time you saw Howard, Tripp?"

Tripp looked at the bookshelves. They were completely full of books and pictures, and some of them had stacks of books on top of the books. He wondered if Pastor Tom had read all of them. He saw several board games on the top shelf, which he hadn't noticed before, including his favorite game: "Clue".

"Tripp? Are you still with me?"

He focused again. "Howard isn't a friend of mine. I mean, I knew him from school, but he got kicked out a while ago and I haven't seen him since."

He worried that Pastor Tom could tell he was lying.

"Sometimes it's best to stay away from certain people. They can get us caught up in things that are best not to be involved with. God loves all his children, but I do recommend that if you do encounter Howard somewhere that you try to keep your distance. Does that make sense?"

He continued to stare at him intently. "Tripp, I'm not kidding. I know some things about Howard that most people don't know. His parents got him involved in things from a very young age that you *definitely* do not want to have any part of."

Tripp wondered what Pastor Tom's meant by "things."

"I would feel a lot better if you'd give me your word that you'll stay away from Howard."

"Ok, yes. I will."

"Good, well that's all I wanted to say about that. So, tell me what else is going on. How's your dad been?"

Another subject that made Tripp uncomfortable. He never really knew how to answer it.

"Oh, he's been good. Haven't seen him in a while. He travels a lot for work."

"Sorry to hear that. You know, our parents are imperfect. They make a lot of mistakes. Mine did too. But at least we know we can count on our heavenly Father when our earthly fathers let us down." He smiled reassuringly.

The idea of a perfect father in heaven sounded very attractive to Tripp, though a little unlikely. Where was He when you needed Him?

Almost as if Pastor Tom read his mind, he answered the question: "The only difference is that we talk with Him through prayer, rather than face-to-face. The good thing about that is that we can talk to Him anytime."

Prayer in church was ok. Doing it at home alone, Tripp always felt as though he was talking to thin air. He knew better than to share this with Pastor Tom. He didn't want him to think less of him.

"Yes, Pastor Tom, I know."

"Do you like fishing, Tripp?"

"I like it ok. I haven't been in a while."

"Great! I'm going to take you fishing, before the water freezes over. I've been meaning to take you out on my boat for a while now."

Tripp did like boats and the water.

With that Pastor Tom stood up and walked around to the front of his desk, and opened his office door. "Bess, are they still practicing?"

Tripp heard her reply that they were almost done. Just then sunlight beamed through the office window and lit up Pastor Tom's chair. Tripp wondered if it was some sort of sign.

"Ok, Tripp, let's go see if your mother has

finished practice. Always nice to talk with you, and we'll get out on the boat sometime next week. Sound good?"

That sounded more than good to him.

He left the room to greet his next appointment in the waiting area. "I'll be right back Bess. Come on Tripp."

They walked into the sanctuary together where his mother was finishing choir practice, and Pastor Tom left Tripp seated in the back to return to his next guest.

C HAPTER 6. SILENCE

Tripp rode home with his mother, replaying the conversation with Pastor Tom. He really didn't feel much like talking, and apparently his mother didn't either, so they rode home in silence. The family had dinner together that night, including Tripp's father, which was a rare occurrence. Dinner was conducted largely in silence as well.

That night, Tripp's sleep was fitful and he continually woke up out of his dreams. He was frustrated, however, that no matter how hard he tried, he couldn't remember the content upon waking. When he started awake yet again, he read 3:12 am on his digital clock. He looked toward the bedroom window, where the bright moonlight made the room appear as though a giant lamp were shining in at a sharp angle. He watched the bare tree branches outside as they swayed in the wind. Because it was so warm the window was cracked open. It was very warm for the December, and Tripp could smell the warmth in the air blowing through the crack into his bedroom. He sat up, pulled the covers off and walked over to the window to look out. The backyard was almost as bright as daytime and the moon was quite large and full. Another swift, fragrant and warm breeze entered the bedroom through the cracked-open window and he felt it blow against his pajama bottoms.

Then Tripp looked down at the backyard and stopped short with a shudder. He squeezed his eyes shut and opened them again, hoping it was his imagination, but there was the profile of Howard sitting at the picnic table in the backyard. Not surprisingly, he was smoking a cigarette and as he exhaled he looked up at Tripp's window. Tripp quickly moved to the side out of sight, but feared he had been spotted. He thought he could detect the smell of cigarette smoke, drifting across the yard and infiltrating the bedroom. He didn't know if he should acknowledge him or just pretend he didn't know he was there. He peered around the edge of the curtain.

Howard was looking toward the back of the yard, but then he turned and looked straight at Tripp's window again. He darted out of the window and got on the floor. Now Tripp was frightened.

He thought of Pastor Tom's last words as he left his office: don't get involved with him. How can you avoid it if he's showing up at your house in the middle of the night? Crawling across the floor to his bedroom door, he turned the handle and opened it. The hallway light was on and the room instantly brightened. He shut the door quickly so Howard wouldn't see the light in his window. Crawling back to the window he peered over the edge of the sill and was shocked to find the backyard now empty. Not a sign of Howard anywhere. He stood up to scan the whole backyard, as well as the neighbors', but there was no sight of him anywhere. He felt a bit of relief, then wondered if maybe Howard had moved to the front of the house. Maybe he was trying to get in. Perhaps the door was left unlocked by mistake? Tripp spotted a lingering sign of Howard's presence: the faint glow of what remained of a cigarette smoldering on the ground by the picnic table.

He opened his bedroom door again just a couple of inches and listened for any sounds. It was completely silent. He thought of going downstairs to have a look around, but a combination of fear and laziness killed that idea. He lay back down in bed, tense, with his eyes wide open staring at the ceiling. He was hoping he could fall asleep again, but between straining to listen for unusual noises in the house and repeated urges to get out from under the covers and to have a look out the window again, he was very restless. He did surrender to the urge a couple of times, though he didn't spot anything out of the ordinary. Apart from the cigarette fully burning itself out, there weren't any further signs of Howard that night.

After a few fitful hours of tossing and turning, the light of dawn began to crack and displace the moonlight. Tripp was frustrated and irritated, tired and anxious. He knew sleep was hopeless and now he would have to face the day with very little of it. He rolled out of bed and walked over to the window to have one last look. Still no sign of him. Checking himself, he knew this wasn't a vision. He hadn't had a vision in some time, and the cigarette butt still occupied its spot. He left the bedroom and went downstairs. The house was still quiet. There was a book open on the kitchen table, but no sign of the reader. Returning to his bedroom he tried to put the haunted night out of his mind and get ready for school.

C HAPTER 7.
GONE FISHIN'

The December warm streak continued into the following week, which was now the start of the school's Christmas vacation. Pastor Tom took advantage of the weather and the time off to fulfill his promise to Tripp.

"So when was the last time you were out on a boat, Tripp?"

"It's been a long time. Probably a couple of years ago, with Dad."

Pastor Tom smiled while he did a couple of short jerks on his line. "Well, we picked a good day to go fishing. They seem to be hungry this morning."

Pastor Tom and Tripp had already caught three fairly large fish at that point, which in Tripp's limited fishing career seemed like a huge haul. He had caught one of them, and Pastor Tom two. Tripp almost lost his pole when his fish suddenly yanked on it. Before the sun came up, there was a chill in the air, but both of them were layered and warm enough even as they sat still in the middle of the lake. As Tripp was waiting for a fish to bite, he began to drift off and his grip loosened on the pole. That's when the fish bit and almost took the pole with him.

Fortunately, he grabbed the pole again and wrestled with the fish to bring him in. The result was well worth it. He brought in a nice big bass. The sun continued its morning ascent over the almost motionless lake, warming them both up, and Tripp began to strip some of his many layers of clothing.

It wasn't too much longer after that Pastor Tom caught two in quick succession.
They were having a good morning and felt full of energy as a result.

"You interested in a snack, Tripp? I brought some granola bars if you're hungry."

"No thank you. I'm ok." He was too focused on catching another fish to be hungry.

"So, tell me more about your dad. Do you see him much these days?"

"I guess. Seems like he travels more than he used to."

"Do you get to spend much time together?"

That was an uncomfortable question. Tripp always cringed when the topic came up, because in his mind the indirect question was whether his father was spending most of his time out drinking. Tripp figured most people knew about his father's drinking, even though it was never directly raised in conversation. The thinly veiled staring, the looks of pity and the conversations in hushed tones when his family would walk in to a public place, were indication enough. The town was relatively small after all, and most secrets could not be held for very long.

"Not so much lately, I guess."

Tripp looked out toward his fishing line. It was completely still. The sun was directly behind Pastor Tom and over his head so that Tripp could barely make out his facial features and had to squint when he faced him. In the silence a gust of wind blew and the boat spun enough to take him out of the direct sunlight.

"We all struggle with one thing or another, Tripp. With your father, it's no different. Just remember that. I'm sure he loves you, even if it doesn't always feel like it."

"I never feel it, because he's never there." He kept his gaze on the fishing line, and away from the eyes of Pastor Tom. He was kind of surprised that came out. His lack of sleep, not just the previous night but over the last several days, had probably diminished his ability to censor himself.

There was no response except another gust of wind, which was a warm breeze, and Tripp realized he was too warm again. He unzipped his fleece jacket and removed another layer.

"Tripp, I'll keep reminding you that God loves each one of us, in spite of the things we struggle with, and the ways we hurt people. He's there for us in all those things, if we let Him be there for us."

Tripp felt mildly comforted by Pastor Tom's reassurances, however doubtful he remained. But he was yanked out of his thoughts by a tug on the fishing line. He sat up at attention and gently pulled the rod backwards. There was another tug on the line.

"Looks like you got another one!"

"I think so," he said as he began to reel it in.

"Reel it in slow and steady, not too quick."

Tripp complied and pulled in his second fish of the day, another bass, a little smaller than the first one, but he was proud of himself, nonetheless.

"Congratulations Tripp. You're a natural." He smiled and grabbed the line, gently removing the fish off the hook and dropping it in the pail of water with the other three.

"Looks like we've got breakfast and lunch!"

Tripp smiled in return, feeling somewhat accomplished as a fisherman. Both of their poles were now on the floor of the boat, and they both laid back on the wooden bench seats to take a break in the warmth of the morning sun. As Tripp looked upwards at the bottomless, blue sky, he noticed a puffy, white cloud drifting toward the sun, threatening to mask it. Another gusty breeze spun the boat a quarter turn, and he spotted darker clouds further toward the horizon. From his position facing upwards he couldn't tell which direction the clouds were coming from. But he was also perfectly content not to know.

"Pastor Tom?"

"Yeah, Tripp?"

"What were you going to tell me about Howard when we talked last time?"

There was silence in response.

Finally, "Tripp, like I said before just be careful with him. There's more going on there than meets the eye."

Tripp knew that all too well. Mr. Tyler's corpse flashed before his eyes. Again, a memory he really preferred not to keep. And once again he felt a tremendous pang of guilt for not doing anything about it.

Tom continued from his reclined position.

"I mean there are things at work here that you are not aware of. It's just better to keep your distance."

Pastor Tom's voice had taken on a serious tenor and he sat up.

"Tripp, do you understand what I'm saying? You're a big boy now, and I know you can make decisions for yourself. I just want to make sure you take me seriously."

Tripp sat up as well and nodded. "Yes, I understand. So, there's something…"

Pastor Tom's pole started sliding toward the side of the boat. He had left the line in the water.

"Whoa, I think I have a biiiigggg one here!" He lurched to grab the pole before it went over the side of the boat and started working it aggressively.

Tripp was left dissatisfied with the Howard conversation, but he let it go as he watched Pastor Tom struggle against the fish.

"This must be huge!" The rod was now steeply curved. Whatever he had on it was heavy. So heavy in fact, that the line snapped, and nothing but the translucent end of the fishing line popped out of the water. The release was so sudden he fell off his bench and onto the floor of the boat.

"Oh no!"

"Oh no!" Tripp agreed. "Are you ok?"

"Haha. Yeah, I'm fine. I wish a got that one though. We could've had dinner too!"

And that was where they decided to end for the morning.

All in all, they had a successful fishing expedition and had enough fish to eat for a couple of meals each. Tripp brought two of them home to his mother, hoping she would know what to do with them. Turns out she didn't, but between what Tripp remembered from Pastor Tom's instructions and his mother's own limited knowledge, they managed to have fish for dinner that evening.

C HAPTER 8.
NEXT STEPS

Tripp knew very little about Howard's background, other than the fact that his parents had died and left him an orphan. Apart from that, he wasn't really sure how he got to be the way he was, however you would describe it. Strange? Yes. A loner? Yes. Evil. Maybe. Pastor Tom would occasionally tell Tripp how wonderful he thought he was. "Such a fine young gentleman," he would say. Sometimes Tripp wondered how two boys of close to the same age and from the same town could grow up to be so different. Tripp worried that maybe he would end up like Howard. Maybe he was already on his way? He just felt like some insecure kid, with not many friends and a messed-up family. At least Howard didn't have to put up with all that family crap. Tripp felt like he had a father who was hardly ever there, and usually drunk when he was home. He said that he would change, but he had said that many times before. It never lasted. Tripp's mom was nice most of the time, but a lot of times Tripp felt she wasn't any better than his father. His sister was ok. She was a bit of a pain sometimes, but ok apart from that.

But then guilt began to emerge. How could he think such awful things? Weren't a lot of the family's problems his fault? He was always getting into trouble himself and worrying his mother. Perhaps things wouldn't have been so difficult between his parents if he had been a better son. He felt the situation was kind of hopeless, and that there wasn't anything he could do to help hold his family together, try though he might.

And there were times when he tried to follow Pastor Tom's suggestion and pray for them. But that seemed even more futile. Tripp never felt like he got a response, and most of the time wondered if anyone was listening. Perhaps God had abandoned him because of his shortcomings? Maybe he didn't have enough faith. It was all so confusing.

He kept thinking of all the times he was the one who started a fight with his parents, or even worse, said or did something that caused a fight between his parents. Like when he would ask for money for the bus or for a school trip, and that would set off a chain of events that ended up with his father and mother screaming at one another, his father storming out of the house, and his mother storming into her bedroom to remain confined there for the rest of the night. This was always followed by a restless night of waiting for his father to come stumbling home drunk, or to not come home at all. If he had only waited to ask, or just found the money somewhere else the whole thing could have been avoided. And so, after a few such incidents Tripp learned to not ask, lest he cause any trouble.

Truth be told, Tripp just wanted his family to be happy and for all them to live together without the fighting and the tension. But he discovered that even when he refrained from engaging in the types of behaviors that he thought triggered these events, they still happened anyway.

C HAPTER 9. LOOKING BACK

When Tripp was older and he looked back at those pre-adolescent and adolescent years, mostly by thumbing through old journals, and partially through memory, he was amazed at how muddled and dark it all seemed. It wasn't at all clear to him what was happening at the time, and it took many years for it to become clear. Muddled, in fact, was putting it mildly. He often felt trapped in his own mind, and it was a dark place to be, full of fear and anxiety. Consequently, he kept a lot of what he wrote in his journal on the positive side, perhaps trying to dull the impact of the pain he was going through. And his memories, likewise, often tried to put a positive spin on things. So, the more time that passed, the less clear it was to him what was real and what was perhaps a sugar-coated memory. That's not unique to Tripp, but human nature. What was unique to Tripp is that he knew the memories were dressed up, and he still felt the dull ache of the reality behind them.

There were a number of things that filled in some of the gaps years later, especially the notebook that was found at the house of Howard's grandmother after she died. Excerpts were even printed in the local paper, *The Daily Chronicle,* and Tripp cut out and kept all of the articles in a shoebox in his closet. The stories were printed on the front page of the paper. They were big news for a pretty small town. Amongst the locals, it was the deep trauma of the treatment by, and death of, his parents that was the most common reason offered as the source of his psychotic behavior. His inability to find firm footing through the stability of a strong family, and the disturbing experiences he underwent as a child, were clearly what led Howard to be who he was today. But Tripp was never so sure, and once he found out the real roots of Howard's behavior, it all made sense.

One of his times looking back on this period, he opened the shoebox up and pulled one of the articles out to read the yellowed newsprint. Here is an excerpt of the newspaper article dated November 20th, from a journal entry of Louisa's dated just weeks before on October 14th:

Here is the journal entry scribbled in the small notebook of Grandmother Louisa during the week before she died, describing a harrowing existence of suffering and neglect at the hands of her grandson, Howard Sandground:

'Howard won't even come to the room anymore even though I call him. He stopped

responding at all weeks ago. Occasionally he gives me something to eat, but he often forgets. I only wish I had been a better caretaker for poor Howard. I know he has had a very difficult childhood and I should have been there for him. I couldn't take care of him the way he needed after they died. I'm sure he is very angry at me for that. I am very weak from hunger and I have run out of water. Based on the days I have counted, this is day 94 that I have been locked in this room and I don't know how much longer I will be able to carry on. I tried my best to show him love. If anyone finds this, I beg you to please go easy on him. All of this is not his fault. I pray someone finds this note and has mercy on him if I am unable to plead for him in person. I pray that God will have mercy on Howard for all the struggles he has had to endure as a child.'

The article went on to explain that Louisa was not found until November 8th, more than three weeks after she wrote her entry, quite decomposed. When the fire occurred and the door to the house was broken though, the putrid smell of her corpse mixed with the smell of smoke in her small two-bedroom house. Howard was long gone.

There was a fire in the house, but that's not what killed his grandmother, and if there hadn't been a fire they may not have found her for months. The mailman had noticed the mail piling up as well, but the normal mail-carrier was home on maternity leave. Her replacement did not think to investigate.

A neighbor noticed the fire and called it in. Fortunately, it was confined to the kitchen and the living room and hadn't spread throughout the house, so they put it out relatively easily. That's when they noticed the smell coming from one of the bedrooms and broke down the door. Within ten minutes four police officers were at the house. The most junior officer of the three that first arrived at the scene turned and vomited when the accumulated stench of a rotting corpse forced its way through the broken doorway and punched him in the face. The other two officers, who had been confronted with this type of scene before, turned to the side and put their shirted arms to their noses to filter the air. The door, broken down, appeared to have been nailed shut from the outside. The junior officer kept his distance and remained by the front door of the house. A television set quietly played commercials in the background of Louisa Sandground's bedroom. She had left it on for company. Apparently, she had died shortly after writing her final plea for mercy on Howard. The coroner estimated that by the time her body was found she had been dead for 18 to 20 days.

CHAPTER 10. HOME SWEET HOME

"Daddy!" she yelled as Pastor Tom opened the front door of his home and she ran to throw her arms around his waist.

"Hi sweetheart! How's my favorite pumpkin today!?" He picked her up and gave her a big kiss on the cheek.

"I'm good, Daddy." She kissed him back. "You smell funny."

"Haha. Yes, I probably smell like fish. I went fishing today."

"Oh, ok." She didn't even pause. "Daddy, can I have a puppy?"

Tom was caught off guard by the question and looked it.

"Uh, I don't know sweetie, you know, puppies are a lot of work." He set her down on her feet and smiled back at her. He still couldn't get over what it was like to have a child love you unconditionally. If only he could do the same, he thought.

He grabbed her hand and started leading her toward the kitchen. "Did you ask Mommy about having a puppy?"

"I did Daddy."

"And what did Mommy say?" As he asked the question he pushed open the swinging door to the kitchen and the subject of his question turned from the sink in his direction.

"Hi honey."

"Mommy said that I should ask you, Daddy."

"Did she now…" He smiled at her, then at his wife, who was still looking over her shoulder in his direction. She smiled back. She knew that her tactic would not work for long.

"Well, Mommy runs the show here, so we have to get her approval before we can do anything."

He winked, and Bess turned back to the plate she had been distracted from. She rinsed it off and set it in the strainer, as their daughter, Rachel, shifted the focus of her efforts back onto her mother.

"Mommy, can we, can we? I'll do all the work. I'll take care of him, and feed him and walk him. You won't have to do anything. You can just play with him if you want to."

Her mother smiled at the sink and continued to wash.

"Well, we'll see sweetheart. Daddy and I will talk it over."

"Okaaaaay," she moaned.

"Why don't you go wash up for lunch?"

"I already did Mommy. See, look." She extended her palms toward her and smiled.

"Well, yes, your hands look nice and clean. Nice job!"

His wife turned as she grabbed the dishtowel to dry her hands. "And how was the fishing?"

"Really good, actually. We both caught some. I have a couple that were worth keeping in the car on ice."

Rachel had left to the living room. "So where did the puppy talk come from?"

She rolled her eyes, "Her friend Lucy got one, and they were playing with it all morning. Now it's all she will talk about."

"Got it. He turned and called to Rachel, "Ok, who's ready to eat?"

"Meee!!!" Rachel shouted as she ran back into the room and sat at the kitchen table.

Bess brought the macaroni casserole from the oven and placed it on the pad in the middle of the table. She added a basket of warm rolls next to it.

"Let me serve you some of that sweetheart." Rachel held out her plate to receive a scoop of hot macaroni and cheese.

"Let me have your plate too honey." She served her husband some as well.

"So, anything on the agenda for this afternoon? Don't play with your food honey. Are you still going to meet with the Wilsons?"

"Yes, I have to pay them a visit today. Robert isn't doing well. The doctors can't figure it out. He's so young too, only 48 or 49, but he seems to be getting worse by the day."

"They don't have any idea?"

"They really don't, that's the odd thing. None of the tests have been conclusive. Anyway, I just prayed with Rob and Samantha for a bit. All things considered, they seem to be in relatively good spirits."

"I'm glad to hear that. Maybe I'll bring some dinner for them tomorrow evening."

"I'm sure Sam would appreciate the help."

"Daddy, guess what?!"

"What sweetheart?"

"I saw an angel today." She smiled.

"Did you now? Where was that?" He looked at her inquisitively.

"I saw him while I was playing with Lucy and Runner. He was watching us just standing by the tree. He was with us for a little while, and then he just disappeared," she said matter-of-factly.

"Oh, really. Well, that must have been very exciting, huh?" Tom wasn't quite sure how to respond.

Bess joined the questioning. "So, what did the angel look like, sweetheart?"

"Well, he was really pretty. And he kind of shined like a light. But not too bright." She thought for a moment. "I didn't see any wings though. I thought angels had wings, don't they Daddy?"

"Well, I don't think all angels have wings."

"How can he fly then? I should have asked him when we were talking."

"Oh, you spoke with the angel?" They both looked at her, now thoroughly intrigued.

"Yeah, we talked for a little bit. Lucy couldn't see him. But Runner was barking at him."

They looked at each other a bit perplexed.

"Oh, and he told me to tell you that Mr. Wilson would be ok."

"He did?"

"Yes, Daddy. That's what he told me."

"Well, I appreciate you telling me Sweetie. Did he tell you anything else?"

"He did say that he could hear me even when I couldn't see him. Isn't it weird that Lucy couldn't see him?"

"Well, I don't know, honey. Probably not. Maybe he only wanted to be seen by you. But it's true angels can hear us anytime. So, Lucy's dog was barking at the angel?"

"Yes, really loud. The whole time. Maybe that's why he left. Runner isn't very big, but he growls pretty loud and scary."

"Yes, maybe so."

"Oh, and when he was leaving, he said to be sure to be watching, because Howard's coming. I'm done, can I go play now?"

Bess and Tom looked at each other in stunned silence.

Tom broke it. "Sorry, honey, what did you say?"

"Can I go play now?"

"No, about Howard?"

"He said Howard's coming. But I don't know anyone named Howard. Do you, Daddy?"

"I do. Nothing you need to be concerned about, but thanks for telling us. And that was everything?"

"Yes, then he left."

"I see. Ok then. Yes, sweetie you can go play now."

She immediately jumped up from the table and ran into the living room.

"Tom, what do you think that was about?"

"I'm not sure. Perhaps it's just her active imagination."

"But where did the name Howard come from then?"

"It's possible she heard someone else talking about him, maybe her friend Lucy or her mother."

"Yeah, maybe."

They finished eating lost in their own thoughts and the topic didn't come up again until that night. As she was sitting in bed reading, she turned to Tom who appeared to be sleeping.

"Are you still awake?"

"Sort of."

"You know I was thinking about what Rachel was saying at lunch today."

He rolled to face her and opened his eyes. "What about it?"

"Well, a couple of times I've been sitting

with her in the kitchen, and I've had the feeling someone else was in the room. I can't really explain it. I didn't see anything, but the feeling was real."

"Well, honey, angels do exist, but you also know she has a very vivid imagination. And it's also not the first time she's said something like that."

"I know. I just remember that feeling. It was very strange. It was a while ago and I forgot all about it until today. It was very sudden and it made my hair stand up. It wasn't a good feeling."

"Well, let's talk about it more another time, ok. I need to get to sleep. I have to be at the office very early tomorrow."

"So what, you're saying you don't believe me?" She looked at him with a hint of indignation.

"No, I'm not saying that at all. I do believe you. I just think we should talk about this in the..."

"Daddy?"

Rachel appeared in the doorway of the bedroom.

"Yes sweetie?"

"There's something scary in my room."

"Sweetheart, you're just imagining things." He rolled back the covers and climbed out of bed to lead her back to her bedroom.

"Daddy, I don't want to sleep in my room. I'm scared."

"Honey, there are no monsters there. You're just having bad dreams."

"No, Daddy, really. They were in my room." She pointed emphatically toward her bedroom doorway, illuminated by the light of the half-moon.

"Ok, honey. I believe you. But let's see if they're still there."

She peered around the edge of the doorway for a moment and Tom walked in and sat on the edge of the bed.

"See there's nothing here now. They left and they won't be coming back, so we can sleep now. The angel you saw earlier is going to watch over you so you can sleep safe and sound, ok?"

She reluctantly stepped into her bedroom. "Are you sure?"

"I'm sure honey. Let's get some sleep, ok?"

"Ok, if you're sure." She climbed back into bed as Tom tucked her in and kissed her on the forehead.

"Only sweet dreams for the rest of the night. Mommy and I are right here," he said as he left her.

"Ok."

He returned to bed.

"All good?"

"All good. She's fine now. Let's go to sleep."

She watched her husband climb back into bed and lie with his back to her. She closed her eyes but was nowhere near sleep. Tom fell asleep almost immediately, and she wrestled against her thoughts as she unsuccessfully tried to get back into her book. The digital clock clicked off the minutes and at some point she lost track, slipping into a fretful sleep.

C HAPTER 11.
LETTERS FROM HELL

It wasn't long after the discovery of the body of Louisa Sandground and Howard's disappearance that Tripp began to get letters from him. He wasn't sure why he didn't tell anyone about them. Perhaps he liked the idea of having a secret. Howard didn't write about what happened before he fled, so Tripp didn't have any more information than anyone else in town. He also didn't use a return address, so Tripp never knew where to write him if he wanted to ask. The post office stamps did provide some clues regarding his whereabouts, but every letter had a different location stamped on it: Boise, Lincoln, DeKalb, Rochester, Detroit, Kansas City. Tripp bought a map of the United States and started placing pins in each location. There were a couple of letters where the location stamps were illegible, and each time, after failing to decipher them, he resigned himself to one less pin. What really struck Tripp was that one letter was stamped locally. He couldn't believe that Howard would come back home and risk being caught in a town where everyone knew him.

It didn't make any sense. Regardless, if he was in town he obviously decided not to stay, because the next one was from Lincoln, Nebraska, two weeks later.

The content of the letters varied. Some seemed written like postcards, with descriptions of what he saw in the town that interested him. In DeKalb he went to a fair and described the roller coaster he rode on. Then other letters were far more serious. He told Tripp that he was thinking of killing someone in the town of Kansas City, because he thought that person was following him. They became progressively more like that, more paranoid, and in some of the later letters, Howard really seemed unstable. He wrote more and more about being followed, and sometimes about having conversations with animals that he encountered in his wanderings. There was a man that seemed to follow him from city to city, but he didn't say much about him beyond the fact that he was following him. As time went on, he wrote more and more about killing others, but he rarely said why, or wrote about having done it. Tripp didn't know if or how often he carried out the threats, but he received a total of about 30 postcards and letters over the course of two years and by the end they were somewhat difficult to understand. Not only did the handwriting become progressively harder to decipher, but the letters themselves became fairly incoherent.

The collection of letters was kept in an old

shoebox at the back of Tripp's closet. They were carefully concealed under some old clothes that had fallen of their hangers and that Tripp never wore. He was proud of how good he was at keeping a secret. Fact is, he did want to tell someone, but he never revealed them and they remained hidden until much later.

CHAPTER 12.
ANTAGONISM

"I hate you!"

She stood firm, stared him down and replied, "The feeling's mutual. I wish I'd never met you. I would be much better off."

"Yeah, sure, like I'm some sort of curse on you. You've done nothing but take from me. I pay for everything and you don't even work. Then I get home and have to listen to you bitch and moan about how miserable your life is. Your miserable life is making mine miserable as well. Why don't you go make someone else miserable and leave me alone."

Now she could no longer maintain her composure, "I leech off you!? You ungrateful son of a bitch! You can't even keep a job without getting fired, and who's the one who always ends up picking up the pieces!? It's me...always me. And how dare you accuse me of not working. I work part-time and then I have another full-time job taking care of you and the kids. You have no idea! I have to work because you can't keep a job for more than six months!"

She tried to force herself to calm down, with mixed success. She knew the children were probably listening, but anger trumped the concern. She watched him as he headed to the closet to get his coat. Out of the blue she started to cry.

"Yeah, right. Like I'm supposed to feel sympathy for you. Not a chance."

She turned away, embarrassed, and slumped on the couch.

"Fine, run off like you always do. Get drunk and pass out at the bar. What else is new?" she sobbed.

He turned to leave without even looking at her. The door was still partially open, and when he opened it wide and pushed the screen door he was startled to find Tripp sitting on the top doorstep.

He stopped dead in his tracks, but only for a moment, then continued out the door, slamming it behind him for effect, then around his son without saying a word and down the stairs. As he opened the car door he mumbled something unintelligible to himself and got in.

Tripp watched as he sat still for a moment, hands on the steering wheel staring into space, then he started the ignition, quickly backed out of the driveway without looking behind. A car traveling down the street screeched on its brakes and skidded to a stop about five feet from the rear end of his blue Chevy. Again, he sat still, the car not moving for several seconds, then finished backing out and drove away. After he was a fair distance down the road the other car continued on as well.

Tripp stared at the empty space his father's car had vacated for a good while, then heard his mother sobbing again. He started watching the ants climb in and out of an anthole on the edge of the slightly crumbling steps, illuminated by the front doorlight. He envied the simplicity of their lives. After a moment he turned to see his mother standing behind him at the screen door. She was no longer crying, but looked disheveled and exhausted.

"It's time for dinner, Tripp. Go get your sister and let's eat."

She turned and disappeared into the living room again.

Dinner was passed in silence. Peas were eaten one-by-one, and the plate remained half-full when Tripp could no longer eat. His mother barely ate at all. Only his sister finished her plate and then watched them both not eat.

C HAPTER 13. ESCAPE

Tripp first met Bubby when he was eight years old. She was out working in her front yard one fall afternoon, raking leaves. He saw her hunched over the rake and came to a standstill, feeling sorry for her as she was clearly struggling with the yardwork. He could see that her back was permanently hunched, so she couldn't really stand up straight. She wasn't making any headway raking the vast number of colorful leaves which had accumulated in her front yard. She turned to see Tripp watching her struggle. He liked the blue color of her dress. It complemented the yellow straw hat.

"Hello zere jung man," she said with a thick accent which Tripp only recognized as an accent but nothing more.

"Where are ju headed?"

"Home, ma'am. I'm walking home from school."

She shuffled a little closer to the white picket fence surrounding her front yard and separating her from the Tripp standing on the side of the quiet street.

"Vud ju like to earn a little money, helping me vith my leaves?"

"Sure, I can help." Tripp was somewhat mesmerized. He didn't even think to ask how much, he just walked through the gate that she opened for him and took the rake from her hands. He didn't care about the money, he just knew he could rake up most of the leaves in a fraction of the time it would clearly take her, and he felt bad for her.

"Ju don't have to rake zem all today, but maybe you can do zat part on ze side?" I vill give ju a dollar. Plus, I'll give ju some nice cookies I made."

"Ok. That's fine."

As she opened the screen door, "Ju can call me Bubby. Just let me know if ju need anyzing."

"Ok, thank you Miss Bubby. I'm Tripp."

And she disappeared in the house, leaving Tripp to start raking.

She returned a couple of minutes later with a trash bag. The area was not large on the side of the house and Tripp was confident he would be done in no time.

"If ju could put za leaves in here ven you finish raking, that vud be vunderfuuul!" She was remarkably grateful for such a small amount of work, and Tripp was pleased he could be so helpful to this poor old woman.

She disappeared into the house again and Tripp finished the section quickly, opening the bag and scooping the leaves into it. When he finished, he looked over the section and was proud of his work.

Not too much later, Bubby appeared in the screen door of her house and called for Tripp.

"Are ju ready for a shnack?"

"Sure." He realized he was starved.

She pushed the door open for him and he entered Bubby's living room. It felt like he was walking back in time, to some era far before he was born. It was neat, but dusty, everything had a brownish-yellow, faded look to it, and the house smelt faintly of flowers and baking bread. A breeze coming through the side window fluttered the curtains which were also a light brown. Framed photographs lined the yellow walls and when Bubby left Tripp to himself, he began to look at them more closely. They all appeared quite old and, not surprisingly, were also yellowed with time. She returned after a few minutes with a tray of milk and cookies. Setting the tray down on the coffee table she fell into the brown and black checkered couch, motioning to Tripp to come and sit down next to her. When he did so she poured him glass of milk to go with the cookies that looked like homemade chocolate chip. Bubby watched him take a bite, like this was the first person she'd seen eat in years. Satisfied that Tripp was enjoying the cookie, she relaxed and poured herself some milk.

"Tripp, vat vud ju like to be ven ju grow up?"

Tripp knew his answer right away, "I'd like

to be a doctor."

"Oh, very nice. Ju vant to make peoples better. Very, very nice."

She took another long, wistful sip.

"Do ju like stories, Tripp?"

"Yeah, sure I do." Tripp leaned forward and sat his glass on the coffee table, staring intently at Miss Bubby.

"Let me tell ju a story 'bout my childhood."

She leaned forward a little bit and began to unfold a distant world.

C HAPTER 14. CAMP

"Ju vill remove every last spot from zese boots. If I see a spot on any of zese boots I vill take jur life and jur mother's life."

The 11-year-old girl kept her eyes down and nodded in the affirmative, all the while polishing away at the black boots lined up on the table before her. The soldier turned and left the dingy, cold room, filled with the toxic fumes of boot black, which the girl didn't notice anymore through constant exposure. She hated the man, all of the men, but she could no longer feel hate, she could only feel numb. She polished away her feelings as she polished away boot after boot.

There was no end in sight, because once she finished this string of boots, she would be expected to begin another, and another. She was all alone in the room, with shelves of shoes, boots, a rough-hewn worktable in the middle, a wooden floor, and two windows where dim, reflected light added a minimal amount of glow to the dark, somber surroundings. It was winter, and the days ended early. But for Belsa, time stood still. She spent most of her days here, alone, though occasionally she would have a co-worker to help, or to work with. The last co-worker was an elderly woman, but long winters, poor nutrition and overwork made her arthritic fingers inflexible. She could not handle the boots or the work efficiently or effectively, and so after three days of working with this woman she did not return and was never seen by Belsa again.

This wasn't the first time this had happened, nor did Belsa anticipate that it would be the last. Several others had come and gone along the way, and she refused to get attached to anyone anymore lest she lose another friend. Friendless was safer; it was always safer to avoid attachments of any kind in a world that constantly crushed hope. She could feel the strain of a tear try to push its way up to the surface, but her eyes remained dry and her heart hardened.

She heard the door open again, and along with a gust of frigid air an old man, with a bad leg, entered the room with a dirty sack slung over his shoulder. She had seen him many times before, but they had never exchanged a word. Likewise, today, he moved across the room in silence and then turned the sack upside down to shake its contents out onto the floor. More boots. When the bag was empty he started to line them up for Belsa to move onto next. Once finished he stood still for a moment and watched her in silence as she continued her work. And after finishing the boot she looked up to catch his gaze. It was only a split second before they broke it off to resume their duties, but the glimmer of connection left her feeling strangely warm and human. It was a short-lived breath of hope in the midst of countless days of empty thoughts and a vacant heart.

As quickly as it arose, it was gone, along with the man.

The boot pair was finished and she moved onto the next one, much larger than the previous pair, and she tried to imagine the man who owned them. Perhaps the fellow schoolchildren made fun of him when he was a boy because of his huge feet. Was he an exceptionally large man as well, or were just his feet disproportionately large? Did he always have such large feet, even as a boy? Belsa thought about her childhood, when she was living a normal life, as a child in school. She liked school, especially math, and longed to study and go to class again. She began to practice her multiplication tables in her mind again as she so often did to make sure she didn't forget them.

$$2x4=8$$
$$3x4=12$$
$$4x4=16$$
$$5x4=20$$

Perhaps she would return to school someday and study algebra. She so wanted to study algebra, but never made it there. Perhaps she could teach someday, teach math to others. Wouldn't that be something? She paused from her work to scratch numbers into the dirt floor with her bony index finger.

6x4=24
7x4=28

She was so absorbed in her computations that she failed to hear the soldier from earlier re-enter the room. She also failed to hear him walk over to her as she scratched numbers into the dirt floor and as he raised his baton over her hunched back. In fact, she remained oblivious to his presence when the baton came down on the back of her head with such force that she was instantly knocked unconscious and onto her face on the floor.

She didn't know how much later consciousness crept slowly back into her mind; just awareness, no sight, no sound, consciousness, then feeling. She felt the cold earth beneath her, then the damp, musty smell of her workplace. Then she realized she was in pain, terrible, terrible pain. A horrendous ache emanating from the back of her head, down the side of her neck and into her right shoulder and back. She tried to raise her head off the ground and the crushing pain made her wince and cry out as she fell back down to the earth and rested her cheek on the earthen floor. The memory of being hit came back to her, and though she never saw what hit her, she knew it was one of the guards because the experience was not a new one. He must have seen her doing her math exercises rather than shining the boots. She lay still and looked sideways at the boots lined up on the floor before her eyes. She lost focus as she stared. After a while it seemed as though the pain in the back of her head was starting to subside. She tried pushing herself off the floor again, and realized she was still in tremendous agony, the piercing pain coursing throughout the back of her head and into her right arm this time. She became faint as she sat up and the blood rushed out of her head. The hatred that she used to feel for the soldiers when they hit her was replaced by a gnawing emptiness, an agitated void searching for an emotion to attach itself to. But the void was too big and engulfed her. She knew the soldier would have just as likely killed her if he had wanted to. If he had hit a bit harder, her life would be over, and he would have thought nothing of it. He would have left her dead and gone home to dinner with his family. Anger served her no purpose here. It only drove her to despair because its subject was faceless and outside the realm of judgment and retribution. When she first entered the camp and experienced a taste of the senseless pain and punishment she suffered, she allowed herself to get angry and even nurtured the feeling, thinking it would keep her spirit alive. But with time the anger turned into hatred, and the bitter roots of hatred began to dig deep down and attach themselves there. She could not hope for the opportunity to seek revenge on those who had hurt her so many times. Their faces constantly changed. To yearn for revenge or justice was a hopeless exercise. It was part of the ongoing struggle between good and evil, right and wrong, but in this version, the struggle was contained within her own mind and the rest of the world seemed immune.

Quite early on it became clear that good would not triumph. So bitterness began to consume her until she found she could taste it in her mouth, and then the stomach pain started. That gnarled hatred served no purpose, because it could never be placed on her oppressors. She would be left holding it forever. It was at that point that the hatred was replaced by a gnawing numbness. In fact, not just the anger, but anything that used to provoke feeling in her would leave her numb. It was replaced with nothing: no anger, no fear, no desire to seek revenge, just emptiness. She felt nothing toward the soldiers. They had become ghosts in a dream, no longer flesh and blood.

Occasionally Belsa would experience a faint shadow of a feeling she used to be familiar with, but it seemed so distant that the thought of trying to pull it to the surface seemed like an impossible task. She would acknowledge its passing and let it drift away. Eventually the feelings floated off on their own before she even noticed them. Most commonly, something resembling fear would grip her, a terror of dying, but she also felt that whatever awaited her beyond this life was probably better than her life now. And so even the thought of death at the hands of her guards left her ambivalent and empty. She would continue to go through the motions of her day-to-day life and avoid thinking about it.

It suddenly occurred to her that the guard may return to find her not working again as she was lost in thought. She pushed herself further up and slowly stood. The pain was not quite as intense now. She swallowed hard and surveyed the progress of her work. She picked up the last boot she had been working on and resumed polishing it with the black-smeared polishing rag. Although she didn't realize it, the work was a comfort to her because it was consistent, with no beginning and no end. Belsa heard the distant sound of laughter coming from outside the shack. She ignored it and polished it away.

CHAPTER 15.
AWAKENING II

Tripp was sitting on the edge of the couch, hanging on every word. He had no idea that such evil existed. He had heard about the Holocaust when reading about WWII in school, but it had never seemed real to him. Even after she finished he was immobilized and he continued to stare at her, unable to believe that someone had lived through that kind of experience.

"Vud ju like some more milk, Tripp?"

"No, thank you. Who was Belsa?" He paused. "Was that you?" He thought he already knew the answer.

"Yes, Tripp, I vas Belsa. I spent many years forgetting, but I vant jung boys and girls like ju to understand vat it vas like. Jung people don't know anymore. And the forgotten past vill repeat itself."

"Oh, yes ma'am. It's horrible. I can't believe that happened to you." He motioned at her small, frail body.

"It vas a long time ago, Tripp. A long time ago. That is vy ve must be careful."

She paused to take a sip from her glass. "Ju

know, Tripp, I can tell some more stories another day if ju like. But today, ve vill have to stop."

"Ok, Miss Bubby. Thank you." Tripp didn't know what else to say.

He stood up from the couch, turned toward the door and made his way while zipping up his jacket. He turned to get a final look at Bubby, a woman he now saw in an entirely different light.

Opening the door he paused and asked, "Do you still hate those soldiers, Miss Bubby?"

"Tripp, I let zat go long time ago. Hate hurts ze hater more zan it hurts ze hated. Come by again tomorrow, Tripp, if ju can. I vill pay ju to rake some more leaves."

Tripp nodded and left her home in the late afternoon sun. He was lost in the world she painted for him and shivered at the thought of being trapped there with no escape. In his mind, he envisioned the scene in black-and-white, the air dry and frigid, with the weak sun struggling to pierce through layers of thick winter clouds blanketing the dusky sky. He wondered if people were living in those kind of conditions today and, if so, where? What leads people to act like that towards others? As he walked home he began looking more intently at the people that passed him on the street. He wondered what lay beneath the layers of clothes and behind the faces and eyes that he passed, men and women. Perhaps their smiles merely masked an evil similar to what Belsa faced. How could one know? People could be mean and unkind to one another from time to time, but this kind of evil was something completely different. They seemed driven to hate by something outside of themselves. Did those soldiers feel guilty for the rest of their lives, or did they forget about it and move on as if nothing had happened? Maybe everyone was capable of committing abhorrent acts, but they presented themselves to the world in a way that made them look like normal people going about their normal lives. Perhaps the world was full of people walking around with a mask on to veil horrific thoughts and actions. Then there are brief instants when the mask is suddenly lifted and the true self emerges. Tripp knew that he was just as guilty of hiding his thoughts as anyone else. Was he capable of such evil as well? Was he at his core as savage as the guards in Bubby's story? He felt a mix of fear, shame and pride in the fact that he knew he was just as capable of such brutal cruelty.

Then Tripp thought of Howard. Howard didn't seem to feel a need to hide anything. He never seemed to wear a mask. He did awful things to people for seemingly no reason, yet he didn't try to hide it. Why? What was it about Howard that he didn't see any need to fit in or to hide his worst impulses from the rest of the world? It was all so confusing to Tripp and he felt a tremendous weight on his heart and mind as he made his way home. History, the history he had heard about in class that went in one ear and often out the other, had now become an all-too-real, first-hand experience, and Tripp felt that he could never view the world in the same way again.

When he walked through the front door of his house his mother immediately could tell something was on his mind. She watched him remove his coat and start heading up the stairs to his bedroom. Before he made it halfway up the stairs she called to him.

He slowly returned to the present after recognizing the voice of his mother and stopped on the stairs. He turned to look at her.

"Oh, hi Mom," he replied somberly.

"You ok, Tripp? Where you been? You're getting home late."

"Oh, no. I just helped someone rake her yard."

"Come sit with me for a minute, will you?"

He walked back down the stairs and sat next to her on the couch.

"So, who was it? Mrs. Anderson?"

"No. It was the old lady who lives on Fulton Street. She goes by Bubby."

"Oh, yes. I know who you're talking about. That was nice of you."

"Yeah, but then afterwards she started sharing a story with me about her experience growing up. It was really awful."

"What experience was that? I know she was in the war."

"Well, yeah, she was a girl, but she wasn't in it

really. She was a prisoner in a Nazi concentration camp. She's Jewish, I guess. I can't believe how cruel they were to her. It's crazy."

His mother paused. "I didn't realize that she was a Holocaust survivor. Wow, that's intense."

"I can't get it out of my head. What an awful time that was. Then I was thinking it seems like we can all smile and act nice, but deep down in the heart, maybe we're all cruel like that."

"Well, Tripp, you have a point. I mean, people are capable of doing awful things. Under the right circumstances, anyone is capable of that kind of cruelty."

She paused again to reflect on what she had just said.

"Well, Tripp, don't spend too much time thinking about it. People are also capable of doing great positive things as well. It's not good to focus on the bad too much. So anyway, tell me what else happened today. Did you have a good day at school?"

"Yeah. It was good. We had a new teacher in math today. Ms. Williams is gone now for some reason. They didn't tell us why, but I like the new teacher."

"That's good. I know how much you like math. All right, well go ahead and wash up. We'll be having dinner soon."

She smiled at Tripp as he headed up the stairs and she went into the kitchen to finish getting dinner ready.

CHAPTER 16. GONE

Tripp's father was gone again. Almost as soon as he returned from his latest work trip, he disappeared. Tripp hadn't seen him, but he knew that he was drinking and he had been gone for two days now.

Tripp had just gotten home from school and his mother and sister were gone too. Usually they were both at home, but there was no sign of either of them. He checked indoors and outside, but no luck. Then the telephone rang.

"Hello?"

"Hey Tripp, it's Daniel."

"Oh, hey Daniel." Tripp felt a little awkward but wasn't entirely sure why. Perhaps it was because he hadn't been his normal self around Daniel or any of his friends lately for that matter.

"My mom wants to know if you want to come over after school tomorrow? She invited you to stay for dinner too. She promised it would be good!"

Tripp smiled into the phone. He wondered what motivated the invitation.

"Sounds good, I guess. I just have to ask my

mom and make sure."

"Ok, I'll see you tomorrow at school then."

"Ok. By the way, did I leave my baseball hat there last time I came over?"

"I haven't seen it, but I'll have a look. If I find it I'll bring it tomorrow."

"Great thanks Tripp. See you tomorrow." And he hung up.

The phone rang almost immediately again, and he pulled it off the hook before he let it go.

"Dan?"

"Good afternoon, is this the Talbot home?" The voice of a man surprised Tripp.

"Uh, yes, it is."

"Could I speak with Tripp Talbot, please?"

"This is Tripp."

"Tripp, this is Detective Winters. I work with the Pittsburgh police department and we have someone here in our custody who has been asking to speak with you."

Tripp didn't know anyone who lived in Pittsburgh, but he suspected he knew who had requested him by name. He hadn't received any letters from Howard in months, maybe close to a year. He had a feeling that something was wrong, but didn't recognize the feeling until now. A part of him was hoping that Howard might simply disappear and he wouldn't have to deal with him ever again. He wondered why Howard could possibly want to speak with him.

"Are you there, Tripp?"

"Uh, yes sir." Tripp's face was furrowed and he stood motionless by the phone waiting for whatever would come next. He felt nauseous.

"Tripp, listen very carefully to what I'm about to tell you, because it's very important, ok?"

Tripp didn't respond audibly.

"Tripp, we found this boy Howard asleep in someone else's apartment here in Pittsburgh. I won't get into all the details over the phone, but there was a serious crime here in Pittsburgh and we believe this boy Howard was involved."

Again, Tripp didn't respond, and the detective continued.

"We arrested Howard and he is in juvenile detention awaiting a trial. As far as we can determine he doesn't have any family or relatives for us to contact, and when we asked him for a contact name, the only person he would mention was you, Tripp Talbot. He has been held here since Tuesday morning. Do you know this boy Howard?"

"Uh, yes sir. I know Howard."

The detective paused for a few seconds, and Tripp heard the sound of his muffled voice talking to someone else, but he couldn't make out what he was saying.

"Tripp, to make a long story short, we've discovered some things about this boy Howard that are troubling. I don't know how you know him, but you're the only other person we've been able to connect him to."

Tripp still didn't know what to say, so remained silent. The letters and postcards he used to receive from Howard were one thing. They were arriving from a safe distance, almost as if he were reading a book or watching a tv program. Detached. But this phone call was bringing the situation too close to home. Tripp felt cornered and scared.

"So, first of all, I would like to pay a visit to you and your parents. How old are you Tripp?"

He finally broke his silence: "Twelve, sir."

"So, I assume your parents are home?"

"Actually, they're not home right now sir. I'm not exactly sure where they are."

"Well, in any event, I'm planning to take a drive out to visit your town the day after tomorrow and I would like to meet with you and your parents. Would that be all right with you Tripp?"

"Sure, that would be fine. I can ask my parents when they get home."

"Yes, I'd like you to do that. I'm going to give you my cellphone number, so have one of your parents call me when they get home, ok?"

"Sure, yes, I can do that."

"Great, you've been very helpful Tripp. Thank you for your time."

"You're welcome, sir."

Tripp took down the phone number and hung up the phone.

C HAPTER 17.
THE MEETING

"I'm Detective Winters and this is Detective Haight." He motioned to his partner. "I want to thank you for taking the time to meet with us today, especially on such short notice."

Tripp's mother nodded. His father was still gone. Neither Tripp nor his mother really knew what the meeting was about, other than the fact that Howard had asked to speak with Tripp and the detective wanted to ask some questions. After the initial introductions were made, the detective asked if Tripp could leave the room and let him speak privately with his mother for a few minutes.

Tripp left up the stairs and stood at the top of them out of sight, so he could continue to listen to the conversation.

"As we mentioned on the phone, this Howard doesn't appear to have any living relatives. The only contact name he would give us was that of your son."

He paused for a response. There was none, so he continued.

"This Howard boy, can you share with us

what you know about him?"

"Actually, I don't know much about him at all. My son interacted with him a few times back when he was here in town, but my understanding is that he ran away a few years ago. Tripp hasn't had anything to do with him since he left. I know his parents died some years ago, so he was living with his grandmother not far from here."

Tripp stiffened at the top of the stairs at his mention. The officer assiduously took notes while the other one seemed to be scanning the living room.

"She died in a fire and they believe it was Howard who set it. It was a tragic story. Apparently, she was locked in her bedroom when the fire burned the house down."

The officer finished scribbling and looked up. "Yes, that is the information we have as well. Apparently, all the relatives on his mother's side have passed away, and his father grew up in an orphanage. We checked and they have no records of his birth family."

He paused to write something else on his notepad. "He also has no birth certificate on record because he was born at home and one was never filed. Our best guess is that he's 15 or 16, so he's a juvenile. Did you know he is accused of multiple murders in several states as well as assaults?"

He looked at Tripp's mother as she nodded an affirmative.

"Well, I know he's been a troubled child and

caused all sorts of mischief, probably involved in criminal activity, but apart from the incident with his grandmother, I'm not really sure what exactly. We read things in the local papers, but I'll be honest, Detective Winters, after he left town I stopped paying attention."

"Yes, I understand. Well, the bottom line, Ms. Talbot, is that we have this boy in custody, but there is insufficient evidence to connect Howard to any of the murders. Also, as this case crosses state lines, the Feds are involved so it's out of our hands. We wanted to speak to you privately before they did."

He paused and looked at the floor. He then asked if he could have a glass of water before resuming. When Tripp's mother returned with one she realized that he was slightly uncomfortable about something. He drank the full glass, set it down and continued.

"There are no eyewitnesses to place Howard at the scene of any of these crimes. The interesting thing is that, well, it's all very strange…" He paused again to clear his throat. "Well, the long and short of it is that none of it would be sufficient to make a conviction stick, so even though he's in federal hands now, they're going to have to let him go." Tripp's mother detected embarrassment.

She broke the silence that was beginning to become a little awkward.

"So, Detective, I don't quite understand. I mean, if there isn't any evidence, I'm not saying it can't be true...I know that the Howard boy is troubled, but maybe he's not the right one? How can you be sure that he actually committed any of these crimes if you don't have any real evidence?"

"That's a good question. The Feds have been tracking Howard for some time now, and he moves about quite a bit. Problem is, whenever there has been an attempt to catch him or place him at the crime, he manages to disappear. He always moves on to another location. When he does though, like clockwork, another incident occurs. And it's often the same scenario: there's a fire, and the victim is locked inside and can't escape."

He glanced over at Officer Haight, who had finished scanning the room and was now listening intently.

"That is until now. In this case in Pittsburgh, we found Howard at the scene."

"You mean at a fire?"

"Yes, at a fire. A fire was called in, and the fire department found Howard seated on the front steps of the house as it burned down behind him."

Tripp's mother tried to visualize the image.

"At first they thought he was a traumatized teenager who lived there and managed to escape. He was taken by ambulance to the hospital and they recognized who he was. At that point he was detained. He's in a local jail in Pittsburgh until the Feds move him. But he's barely spoken a word except to ask for Tripp."

For the first time in the conversation she

became animated. "Ok, now wait a minute here. I really don't want my son getting caught up in all of this. He's had nothing to do with Howard in probably two or three years. Maybe longer. And he's far too young to be dragged into some sort of investigation."

She took a deep breath and continued, "We're glad to provide you with any information, but I'm not sure we can do much beyond that. I'm not even sure that would be of much help. Like I said, Tripp hasn't seen or had any interaction with him in years. I'm sure you know a lot more than he does at this point."

"I understand your concern, ma'am. We would still like to speak with Tripp if that's ok with you."

Detective Haight added, "The federal authorities are going to want to speak with him as well, so it may be better if we speak together with him first. But it's up to you."

"That's fine. You want to speak with him now?"

"That would be great, ma'am if that's possible."

She walked over to the bottom of the stairs and called out to him. It was pretty obvious he had been listening to the whole conversation because he immediately replied over the railing at the top of the steps.

"Tripp, can you come down and speak with the officers here for a minute."

"Ok," he said as he headed down the stairs.

He and his mother seated themselves next to each other on the couch.

"Tripp, I'm Detective Winters and this is Detective Haight. I spoke with you on the phone a couple of days ago."

"Yes, I remember."

"Tripp, we've been chatting with your mother and we could use your help. I know Howard wanted to speak with you directly. You two seem to have a special relationship."

He said it half as a statement, half as a question. Tripp didn't know how to respond. For him his interaction with Howard was a lot like reading a piece of horror fiction. For a long time now, Tripp did nothing more than read and collect Howard's letters, and nobody knew about the letters, regardless. Apart from that there hadn't been any interaction. The fact that Howard was asking to speak with Tripp broke that dynamic, and Tripp still wasn't sure how to respond to it.

"Tripp, we think we can use that special relationship you have with Howard to prevent any other crimes from happening."

Tripp and his mother looked at each other.

"Honestly, sir, I don't really have any relationship with Howard. I know he left town and I haven't had any interaction with him since. I'm not sure why he asked for me."

"Tripp, we know about the letters you've been receiving."

Tripp was dumbfounded and speechless, as well as caught. He could tell his mother was staring him down.

"Tripp, what is Detective Winters talking about? What letters?!"

He remained silent and looked at the floor.

"Tripp, answer me! What is he talking about? Have you been writing to Howard?"

Her eyes remained on him, then he looked up at Detective Haight who was also watching him carefully.

To this day Tripp didn't know how the police found out about the letters. He never asked.

He responded to Detective Winters. "Yes, I did. I, um, yes, Howard wrote me a few times. But I never wrote him back."

His mother was audibly upset.

"Where are the letters now?"

"They're in my closet.

"Go get them and bring them down here!"

Tripp immediately ran upstairs and surfaced the box from the back of his bedroom closet. He brought it back downstairs to the living room and handed it to his mother. She was surprised at the weight as she took it into her lap to open it.

"This is more than a few, Tripp. How long has this been going on?"

"Pretty much since he disappeared, a couple of years ago, I guess. I mean, well, that's when I got my first letter. But he stopped writing a while ago."

His mother let out another sigh of frustrated shock.

"Why didn't you tell us?"

"I didn't think...I mean, I didn't think it mattered, really. He keeps moving...and, the letters don't really say anything."

He knew right away that his excuses were making things worse. He stopped talking.

His mother let out a groan, "So that's what that map in your bedroom is, isn't it? You've been keeping track of him."

"Yeah. But I never knew where he was because by the time I got a letter from one place he would be in another. Every letter is from somewhere new. I never knew where he was or where he was going."

He followed up with, "So you haven't been in touch with him, apart from these letters, since he disappeared?"

"No, never."

"Have you kept all of them? Are these all the letters here?"

Tripp nodded. "Yeah, they were all in this box in my closet. I kept all of them in there."

"Can we have a look at the map as well?"

Tripp ran up the stairs again and came down a few minutes later with the whole corkboard with a map tacked to it and colored pins dotting towns and cities across the country.

"Officer, I'm sorry, I had no idea this was going on. Tripp, tell the officer where these letters came from and what they're about. We need to know about all your contact with Howard. All of it. No more secrets!"

"Really, I mean it! There's nothing else."

He looked at Detective Winters and then turned to Detective Haight. He was still standing, watching the interaction unfold, expressionless. Tripp turned back to Winters who had received the box from Tripp's mother and was rifling through its contents.

He wanted to make sure they were convinced he was telling the truth. "Honest, I swear. This is everything I have. I've told you everything."

Winters looked satisfied and stood up. "Tripp, we're going to need to take these letters and your map as evidence. I hope you understand."

"Yes sir."

"By the way, Tripp, Howard has written other people as well."

He wondered who else he could be writing, and he came up blank.

"Ok, Tripp, go to your room while I work this out with the officers. I'll deal with you later."

"Tripp we still may need your assistance. I will make arrangements with your mother. And thank you for your help today."

Tripp nodded and gladly went back upstairs to get out of the hotseat. Going into his room he lay on his bed and stared at the fluorescent green glow stars and planets he had stuck on the ceiling many years before. He could hear the indistinguishable sounds of the continuing discussion in the living room. He felt guilty for keeping the letters a secret, but he also felt relieved that he no longer had to.

Officer Winters took the letters that he had placed on the coffee table and carefully placed them back in the box. He thought they might be in some sort of order, and he didn't want to disturb it. He and his partner put their hats on while walking toward the front door. At the door Winters reached into his shirt pocket and pulled out a small pad of paper and a pen. "I'm going to leave my contact number. Don't hesitate to reach out if anything comes up or you have any questions. Once we review the letters we'll be in touch again."

He handed her the folded sheet of paper, opened the front door and they left. She watched from the front window as they backed out of the driveway and drove away. She suddenly shuddered. All she wanted was for this whole thing to disappear.

After they were blocks away, she turned and entered the kitchen. As she sat down at the kitchen table she caught her image in the darkened window over the sink. Her hair was disheveled. Drained, she stared at the wall and thought about how she needed a stiff drink, or a few. Then she thought of her husband and put it out of her mind. A deep chill went through her and she shuddered again.

C HAPTER 18.
SHADOWS

The streetlight was out. It looked like someone had thrown a rock at the frosted lamp encasement, breaking the bulb within. Howard didn't notice. He was staring at the ground as he made his way down the deserted street, filled with damp dusk. The air was cold, but not frigid. Again, he didn't notice even though all he was wearing was a t-shirt. He took a drag on his cigarette and stared at the ground ahead of his pace.

"Fuck those assholes. Ain't no one worth a shit anyway. I'll kill them all if I have to."

He was seething. His chest was tight, clenched into knots with pure hatred. All he wanted to do was take his anger out on those around him. The world was against him. Always had been and he didn't care. At least that's what he told himself. He used to think at times that it was unfair, but then he would keep telling himself that there is no such thing as fair. Things were what they were. The world had no obligation to him, and he had no obligation to the world or its inhabitants. Except to carry out his mission. That, at the end of the day, was all that mattered.

Though from the outside he often appeared locked in his own mind, trapped even, he continually assured himself that he was completely free. He could do exactly as he pleased and he didn't owe anybody anything. He nurtured this belief that the emptiness of life, and his acceptance of that fact, made him unique; one of the few that were actually free. His parents taught him this well. He had no feeling for them either, or perhaps he did, but it was a mild revulsion mixed with determined indifference: when they came to mind, he would deliberately choose to think about something else. They were gone now, and they weren't a part of his life when they were alive except to direct him toward his mission. His grandmother was another story. In his weaker moments, when he couldn't muster enough anger or apathy, he was tortured by a deep guilt gnawing away at him. Most of the time it was subliminal, but on rare occasions it was not.

When his parents were gone, Howard's grandmother took him in and even though at that young age he was already fully dedicated to destroying whatever crossed his path, she continued to love him no matter what he did to her. He made a concerted effort to get her to stop, but she refused to give in. Ultimately, he knew what he needed to do. He always knew what he needed to do. The Voice would make it very clear. It would often be faint at first, but it would always grow in volume over time.

Howard had begun to recognize the Voice at an early age, so now he didn't even try to ignore it. He knew it was futile because eventually it would get so loud that he could no longer function. It would consume him. With his grandmother, he did try to ignore it. He would not kill her. Surely there had to be another way. But it persisted. It persisted wherever he went, whatever he was doing, any time of day or night. The volume would grow, eventually drowning out all other voices. It simply said, "Kill her." And Howard continued to refuse. As the volume grew louder he would get horrific headaches, and nothing would take them away. He tried to think how he could satisfy the Voice without killing her. Perhaps if he locked her in her room, so he couldn't get to her, it would give up and leave for now. He couldn't even think straight at this point because the command was so loud and invasive and persistent that he could no longer sleep nights. It came from deep within his skull. He was desperate. He found the hammer in the basement, and a jar of nails, and while she was asleep in the middle of the night, he put twelve nails into the door and the jamb. She couldn't get out, but he could no longer get in either, so he couldn't harm her even if he wanted to.

The Voice disappeared. But only for a brief time. Then it came back with a vengeance. He curled up on the floor and squeezed his head, screaming no. Days of no sleep, and no peace. He tried to distract himself, but knew it was of no use. This would never end until he did as he was instructed. He could hear his grandmother calling from the other side of the door to her bedroom, pleading for Howard to help her, but he could barely hear her voice over the din.

And then he knew he had no choice but to do what it said, just as he always had. Yes, he had no choice, because this torture would never end. There was only one way to do it as well: he would light the house on fire. And that's exactly what he did.

He continued to hear her calling to him as he went to his bedroom to gather a few things; as he pulled out a book wrapped in a cloth and stuffed it into his backpack, along with another shirt and the money hidden in his dresser drawer; as he calmly walked back to the living room; as he pulled out his cigarette lighter and lit the bottom of the living room curtains on fire. He lit each one separately in the living room, then did the same thing to the kitchen curtains, finishing with the curtains in his bedroom. The curtains were old, dusty and crepey and erupted in violent flames almost instantly. As he left his room the living room was now fully ablaze and spreading, with smoke starting to blanket the house. Ignoring the calls of his grandmother, he walked out the front door and a little over two miles to the interstate. He hitched a ride on the onramp with a non-local who had pulled off to gas up. He didn't care where he went, as long as it was away. As soon as he had left the burning house the Voice stopped. The rush of silence was deafening.

His grandmother had no idea what was going on. She knew her grandson had trapped her in the room, that she could tell, but knew nothing else. The window to her bedroom was small, and it was jammed by years of house settling. It was also paned, and although she managed to break through a corner of it, it wasn't nearly large enough for her to climb out, especially as frail as she was. By the time she did break the window, smoke had started filling the room faster than it could escape through the broken glass and it wasn't long before she passed out on the floor, never to regain consciousness. As it was still the middle of the night, it was close to thirty minutes before any neighbors woke and saw the fire. They immediately called the fire department, but it was far too late. Most of the house was engulfed in flames at that point, and Louisa Sandground along with it.

These memories flashed before Howard as continued his seething walk down the street in the cold, damp night. He thought back to that night when he walked away from his grandmother's burning house. He remembered it being nearly a full moon, though not quite. The dreadful pain of guilt ran in waves through his body, but he told himself that he had no choice, and he did everything he could from that point on to banish guilt from his thoughts. He hadn't experienced it Mr. Tyler or any of the others. Those were easy. But when he had to kill his grandmother, for the first time in his life, he felt like something was crushing him under inexorable, suffocating weight while ripping his body apart.

Now he could only faintly remember that feeling. He hadn't experienced it before that night or since and that was years ago. Never again did he try to ignore that Voice. He knew from that day on it was a losing battle, and whatever it told him to do, he did, without resistance or delay.

He stepped in a puddle that he didn't see in the darkness of night. It was cloudy now, no moon projecting light, and there were no streetlights on the outskirts of the town. He felt moisture seeping into his sneaker and sock.

"They'll pay. I'm going to make ever fucking one of them pay. Everyone." He was barely audible.

Howard led a charmed life. He was seventeen now, but he had so far avoided getting caught for any of the crimes he committed. He had been leading a life of death and destruction for several years now, on the run even longer. His parents were gone, his grandmother dead. He disguised himself well and was always moving. He was large for seventeen, and years of hate and killing had aged him. He had no problem passing for an adult of twenty, and even older. He never stayed in one place more than a few days and never returned to the same town. He also avoided small places where he would immediately be recognized as a stranger.

He was on a mission. He had no idea what the ultimate goal was and no idea how long it would last, but he knew for certain he was on one. He was clearly being guided by the Voice. Usually it was the same, but occasionally it sounded like his dead mother or father. They had dedicated Howard's life to whatever was behind that Voice, and he was going to do whatever it told him to do. He had faith it was in his best interest.

The fact is, at this point, Howard had nothing to lose. He had nothing. The only person he trusted was Tripp though he didn't know why. He was also convinced that Tripp was integral to his mission. Tripp was the only one he would speak with, and he took it as his responsibility to protect Tripp.

"Fuck them," he spittled as he heard a car coming from far behind. He got off the road to hide in the tall grass until it passed. His dialogues with himself were usually a stream of expletives directed at everything that came to mind, including his dead parents. Once the car was out of sight he re-emerged and continued to wind his way along the dark and desolate streets. As he started to approach the lights of another mid-sized town, he saw a homeless man across the street at an intersection, sitting on a milk crate. Something putrid hung in the air of the intersection, hung on the chill. He thought of grabbing a broken 2x4 lying on the side of the road and hitting the homeless man across the head to put him out of his misery, but he just continued onward, ignoring him altogether. The man called out to Howard, some gibberish that Howard had neither the patience nor the interest in trying to decipher. He only cared about reaching his destination at this point. His rage was all he was aware of at the moment. Lately he was always either angry or numb. Something inside of him fed the anger, and when the feeding stopped, he went numb.

The streetlights and stores along the main street in the town lit up the faces of the couples and families leaving the restaurants and bars. He ignored them and turned the corner at a brick building, continuing on for another twenty minutes or so. The street became progressively more desolate until he turned into an alley and approached a large metal door of an abandoned warehouse covered with graffiti. Using a tapered piece of rusted metal lying where he had left it on the ground he slipped it between the door and the wall to pry it open. The large, bare room inside contained a mattress in the corner and a large pile of garbage and wood along the wall. There were the remains of a fire that had been burning in the middle of the floor. Charred wood still glowing from fire embers and blackened newspaper remnants were all that were left of it. Behind the bed was his backpack that contained some more clothes and the book he brought with him when he began his journey, wrapped in cloth and buried in the bottom. It was the only possession of any significance that Howard kept.

When he started on his mission years earlier, it was the killing itself that made him feel alive. He used to cherish that feeling. Even if it was an ant, crushing life was exhilarating. Then one day, not too long ago, when he was about to kill an older man, out of little more than a desire to feel alive again, he realized that he couldn't feel anything. As he stood over his latest victim, waiting for the surge of emotion to come, he found himself nothing but numb and empty. His victim lay on the floor, still conscious, screaming and writhing in pain, but Howard was consumed with confusion about his lack of emotional response. He left the victim, who did eventually die without a finishing blow, and walked out of the house by the back door while trying to process this new experience. As he roamed the city streets in that early night, his raw exhilaration grew as he realized his metamorphosis was now complete. His capacity to feel was gone forever. He knew that day would come, but he did not know how or when. He saw the progression over the years, but now his transformation was complete.

His whole life, Howard was doing things human nature is naturally repulsed at doing, and he had to silence his conscience, crush the anxiety, the guilt, the sadness. Yet it persistently emerged, at least to some degree, and nagged him. So he tried even harder to root it out.

That was until today. Today, finally, there was no feeling at all. It was as if he was the observer of the show of his life, or more accurately, a historical account of his life and actions, devoid any emotional content. He had finally reached the next stage.

He shut the door behind him and slid the lock on the inside of the door in place. There was only one large, grated window in the room, which had been painted over in black. It let enough dusk light seep in to see the outline of the contents of the room but not much more. He grabbed a piece of newspaper and inserted it under the remaining wood in the middle of the floor. He then scanned the floor by the mattress until he found the open pack of matches and grabbing them, lit one to the newspaper sheet. It took a few tries, but eventually the room began to glow with the light of the small fire. He added a piece of charred cardboard which also struggled to carry the flame to the wood above it.

Howard sat down on the edge of the mattress and grabbed his backpack. He pulled out the wrapped book from the bottom of the bag and clutched it to his chest as he laid back and stared up at the ceiling, thinking briefly about his parents, the ones who had always taught him the truth. They had lived it themselves and had raised him with it. His parents were banished from the human race, left to live out their remaining years sowing death and destruction in their wake, and thereby Howard's wake as well. But that's the price of knowing the truth. Perhaps they paid dearly for it--ultimately with their lives--but it was worth it. Howard believed he was smarter than that. In fact, he was. Although few would have guessed it by looking at him, Howard was brilliant, and he used his intelligence to his advantage. He had outside help, no doubt, because as a child also banished from the human race he was given a mission, and his master looked out for him to enable him to fulfill that mission. But he was a genius regardless. As mentioned before, he had no clarity around what the end purpose of his life was, but he didn't need to know. He knew there was one, as long as he did what the Voice told him, everything went fine.

Howard looked again at the wrapped book in his hands, then laid it on the floor. He smiled, an extremely unusual thing for Howard. He was doing what he needed to do, and he was doing it faithfully. But then the smile evaporated. For a brief moment there was an acute sense of loneliness, and then just as quickly it was gone and the anger returned. Loneliness wasn't real and there was no room for that. He had the ultimate source of power in his knowledge and freedom. But then where did the fleeting disconnection and isolation come from? The best he could do, because he didn't have an answer, was to ignore the question and to nurture the anger instead.

He would just continue to act as instructed.

His parents forged his path, armed with the same knowledge that they imparted to Howard, and living with the same freedom that comes from not being a member of the human race. Humans often don't realize all the constraints and barriers the human condition throws up in our paths. Howard was free of every single one of them. He would not suffer the fate of his parents, dying senselessly at the hands of those who were ignorant and knew no better. He was better than that. His parents sacrificed Howard to this freedom. They willingly gave him up, and once they had, they then raised him and instilled in him the values that would enable him to live a life somewhere between this one and the next one. He saw things that others would never see, and they lived their lives at peace with their delusion. He despised them for their ignorance, and their ignorance of their ignorance.

What baffled Howard was the realization that some people preferred to live in the artificial construct of their lies, even though they were smart enough to see the truth. They were more comfortable living life as a lie, because most people couldn't handle the truth. The craven belief that there was something out there that was taking care of us, that had all of life's circumstances in the palm of its hand, was so attractive that even an incontrovertible proof that this was a falsehood could not shake that attraction. The knowledge that he, and he alone, knew the truth, and that he was comfortable embracing it, gave him a profound sense of superiority. He winced another smile, not a full smile, but a smile of arrogant pride, stifled by the rage that constantly brewed within him. He exhibited absolute indifference to those he came in contact with from the outside world, but the predominant emotion that constantly rippled below the surface was one of rage. He reflected on his rage for a moment; or it would be more accurate to say that he reflected on the surge of raw energy that flowed within his chest. He didn't identify it as rage or anger anymore, but simply as raw energy that motivated him to keep going when he no longer was inspired to act. That energy had a source from without that kept it burning.

There were rare moments when he had acted with uncharacteristic kindness toward another; and he couldn't justify or explain the reason for this behavior. The compassion he felt for Tripp, for example, when he discovered that he was being abused by his teacher Larry Tyler. He couldn't even identify it as compassion, it was more hatred, but it was in response to the mistreatment of Tripp, i.e., there was a reason behind it, derived from a just cause. Tyler was an animal and he deserved what he got. It wasn't a moral calculation, even though his initial response was rage and a desire to avenge Tripp. No, Howard was simply removing vermin as an exterminator would.

Compassion was unusual, and unnecessary, for Howard. His rage was a natural instinct, and it did not need a source, it was a primal response. Yet it struck him as strange, because when he didn't feel apathetic or numb toward the world around him, he usually experienced that raw energy as hatred and rage. He rarely experienced anything approaching compassion, never mind the concept of love.

It hadn't always been that way. He remembered when he was younger, when he was much more conflicted. He already knew who his master was, but there was still a part of him that wanted to be a member of the world he lived in. He didn't try to fit in in school, but he hadn't completely abandoned himself to being hopelessly locked out of the circle of human life. That came later. He remembered the first day he met Tripp at school and had a conversation with him. Tripp didn't laugh at him like the other kids did. He could have beaten the mockers to death if he wanted to. He was infinitely larger and stronger than them, but for the most part he simply chose to ignore them when they laughed behind his back. Tripp, however, didn't purposely avoid him and even said hello to him when they crossed paths. When Howard came home from school that day he was excited to share with his mother that he had made a friend at school. He expected some sort of words of affirmation, but what he received instead was a severe and brutal beating, and a warning that he must never allow himself to connect with others.

He was not like them and never would be. In the course of the bloody blows he received he stopped feeling the pain and let the desire go. He had a greater purpose in life and he made that the only thing that mattered to him. She told him if she ever found out he was making friends, she would beat him unconscious. Howard heard this just prior to falling unconscious via a blow to the neck. It was at that moment that he resigned himself to being separate.

From that day forward Howard's trajectory was clearly set, and he began to engage in ever greater forms of criminality and delinquency. His expulsion record from school was the first clear indicator. Years later, when Howard's parents thought he was in a position to understand the full weight of the truth, they laid it out for him. They walked him through their discovery, their re-birth and transformation, and the fact that they had committed Howard's life to the same fate from the moment of his conception. Howard was born into this destiny. The text, the very text that Howard had clutched to his chest just moments before, was a tangible manifestation of that fact. At the age they opened his eyes, he didn't fully grasp the truth, but that didn't matter. It had to be violently imposed on him until it became all he knew and lived. The implications of that reality became progressively clearer to him over time. Eventually, the appropriate course of action became instinctive, but it still didn't always come naturally. There was an incident when he was young, probably seven or eight, when his mother was being arrested in their home. Howard heard yelling in the kitchen and then heard his mother screaming. He crept out of his bedroom and into his favorite hiding place in the living room to see three men in suit and tie putting her in handcuffs and leading her out of the house through the kitchen door. Howard was conflicted, as his instinctive response was to defend his mother, and to get the shotgun hanging in the garage to shoot these men in her defense. But they always taught him he should never risk his own life to help another, that he should never become attached to anything or anyone emotionally, and in the end all that mattered was that he remain faithful to the mission. Of course, for a young boy, defending his mother is the most primal and instinctive thing to do, but he fought it off and remained hidden while she was escorted out of the house and they drove away. That was his first major test: regardless of what his instincts screamed at him to do, he wasn't going to listen to them. The mission always came first.

Whenever something did occur that put strain on that supposition, he quickly disposed of it from his mind. At some point he came to the realization, and this made him feel smug, that maybe remorse or fear was simply something left over from the evolution of the animal kingdom, something deep within the brain stem that needed to be rooted out. And besides, he knew that any feeling at all, especially sympathy, guilt and love were all as meaningless as life itself. Case closed.

In spite of his passing the test, however, it turns out that he didn't escape notice completely. One of the three men that had taken his mother away had remained at the house and was standing at the back of the driveway when Howard emerged from his secret hiding place and opened the front door. The officer immediately noticed the door open and began walking toward the front steps. Howard slammed it shut and locked it, not sure what to do next. The officer gently knocked on the door. Though his voice was muffled, Howard could hear him.

"Hi there, young man. We didn't know you were home. We're not here to hurt you and we're not going to hurt your mother."

Howard remained still as he listened.

"We had to take your mother to the police station to ask her some questions. That's all." A long pause.

"Your name is Howard, right?"

Howard didn't respond.

"Well, Howard, we would like you to come to the police station as well and you can see your mother there. Would that be ok with you? I'm Officer Young by the way."

Howard thought about it, and in the end believed him. Besides there wasn't much else he could do. He reopened the front door.

"Thank you, Howard. Again, we're not interested in hurting you or your mother. We just want to ask her some questions. Let's take a ride to the station."

Howard locked and pulled the door shut behind him, following the officer to his car parked on the street a couple of houses down. The officer opened the front door for him and asked him to have a seat. Shutting the door after he climbed in, he walked around the back of the car and got in as well, phoning the station that Howard was accompanying him.

Howard stared out the window and watched the neighborhood pass by as they made the short, ten-minute drive to the station. Once there, the officers tried to make his time enjoyable, letting him watch whatever he wanted on the television and giving him a Snickers bar.

After some time, there was a woman who came to meet him, and she took him to a side waiting room with another officer. She did most of the questioning. She was gentle in her approach, but Howard divulged absolutely nothing. Though they thought he was protecting his mother, the truth of the matter is he had nothing to divulge, because he really didn't know anything about the accusations. He also had no idea where his father was, which wasn't unusual. He would sometimes vanish for weeks at a time. He thought nothing of it.

After she finished asking him questions, the two of them left and a short, chubby white officer with a slight limp, came in and gave him another choice of candy bars. He deliberated for a few seconds then grabbed the Hershey's chocolate bar out his hands. The officer paused and smiled, then sat down next to Howard. He opened his own candy bar, took a bite, and chewed thoughtfully as he stared at the wall in front of him. After ingesting the energy from his first bite, he began.

"Howard, this must be hard, huh? I mean you don't know what's going on with your mom, do you? It can't be easy to see your mother get arrested like that."

Howard looked at the officer and paused mid-bite while he replayed the episode in his mind. In truth, he didn't know what he felt, if anything.

Howard finished his bite and swallowed, then asked the officer what she had done wrong.

"Howard, your mother is suspected of a few things, but at this stage they're what are called allegations, so we're not sure yet if they're true or not. We just brought her here to ask her some questions so we can get to the bottom of it. I'm sure everything will be fine."

Howard nodded, but the officer didn't seem to believe what he was saying, and Howard didn't either.

"Anyways, you and your mother should be able to go home shortly." He patted Howard's knee as he stood up. "Just sit tight, partner. It won't be much longer."

Howard watched him limp out the exit.

The officer was wrong. Howard sat for three more hours in that room. It wasn't long before he began to get bored and noticed that there was a remote control sitting on a table in the corner. He hoped it operated the television hanging on the wall next to the door. He tried switching it on. He failed and stood up to bring the remote closer to the television. It worked, and the room filled with the canned laughter of a sitcom he had never seen before. It was a relief to have the noise to break the silence. Howard continued to stare, now at the television, but his mind was lost in a perpetual playbook of the events of that day. He wasn't sure how long he had been at the station, and there were no windows in the room so he didn't even know what time of day it was. He was in this room for the timespan of several television shows and the beginning of a news broadcast. He wasn't paying much attention until the news suddenly took an unexpected turn. His mother and father were both the subject of a headline story. This wasn't the first time his parents had been accused of being involved in some sort of criminal activity, but he didn't recall ever seeing it on tv. As he sat alone in the waiting room he felt a knot twisting in his stomach. By this age, Howard had already been exposed to countless traumatic episodes at the hands of his parents. More than most individuals experience in a lifetime. He was used to feeling ashamed and even guilty himself when his parents were caught or made a public spectacle.

Both his mother and father were accused of killing a wealthy couple days before in one of the nicer areas of town. The report didn't provide too many details, but they did acknowledge that his mother had been arrested and was being held, while his father was still at large. Howard had witnessed his parents take another person's life before, in a brutal incident that doesn't warrant a recreation here. In spite of that, Howard still didn't think his parents were killers. Later, when Howard held the body of another human being as he breathed his last breath, and Howard saw the life of that individual slip away, he knew, that it was all too easy to take another person's life. Like some sort of morbid epiphany, something in Howard clicked and the idea of taking another person's life was no longer an inconceivable event to him. He took that person's life by simply pulling the trigger on a gun aimed at the man's chest. He didn't intend to shoot the gun, but that was beside the point. After he realized what had happened he dropped the gun and lifted the man up by the armpits, trying to shake the bullet out of him. But he saw, unequivocally, the fragility of human life in that moment, and how utterly simple it was to take it away.

Later, when he reflected on the incident, that knowledge made him feel powerful. He found it amazing that human beings managed to avoid the inevitable fate of death much sooner than they did. Howard himself often wondered why it was that he hadn't faced his own death much sooner, especially when he saw his parents dance with it like it was some sort of game. What in the world was keeping him alive? His parents put him in countless situations that should have guaranteed his demise. Yet, even though it seemed like his parents cared little about whether he lived or died, Howard survived.

Howard wasn't really listening to the television news anymore. He saw a spider fall by a strand from the ceiling and climb its way back up to its webbed home in the corner behind the bracketed television. He was mesmerized. He tried to enter the world of the spider and his mind went an inky black, which then turned into a hot orange. It was the fire he had lit which now consumed the house behind him. He was tired. He still believed in the mission and he would still follow the commands of the Voice, but he needed to rest. He sat on the steps and listened to the crackling of the wood beams behind him. He couldn't move. He was so tired. He knew he had to keep on, but no, tonight he couldn't move another foot. He wasn't just tired, he was completely drained of every last ounce of energy. This surprised Howard. He had never felt this way before. Always the rage came and pushed him onward. But tonight the rage didn't come. Tonight nothing came. He simply sat, and waited, while the heat of the flames pounded his back. The Pittsburgh Fire Department and Police didn't make him wait long. He was first treated as a patient, then as a criminal, and placed in jail. He had no energy left to care. He spent several days in jail, then, as usually happened, the Voice guided him out through an inadvertently unlocked door. He was well rested and on the move again. The Voice always drove him, but also took care of him.

Howard was drawn out of his reflections by the coldness now beginning to consume the abandoned warehouse. He sat up on his dirty mattress and saw that the fire in the middle of the room had almost gone out. He added wood and some paper trash to it and got it going again, then laid back down. He tried to return to where his thoughts had left off, but the inky black of the spider's world consumed him and he fell asleep.

C HAPTER 19. AWAKENING III

At some point in nearly every child's upbringing, they become familiar with a certain collection of stories, some mythological, some historical. To the child, the two are usually indistinguishable. Many of these stories have elements that are consistent across geographical and cultural boundaries. The characters and the settings may vary a little or a lot, but the theme of the story is universal.

One example is the story of Genesis: Adam and Eve in paradise, the Garden of Eden, the dawn of humanity. The creation narrative has multiple variations on the theme, but the central plot remains the same, and it goes something like this: In the beginning God created the heavens and the earth, and the creatures that roamed its lush and fertile landscape. God desired the love and fellowship of conscious living beings, with souls and choices of their own. God knew that it was far more fulfilling to be loved by those who chose to love you, than by those who have no choice. Therefore, God created mankind, and from him womankind.

In the Hebrew Bible, known widely throughout the western world, the man was named Adam and his female companion, Eve. In that same version of this narrative, these two prototypical human beings made their home in the Garden of Eden, an unspoiled earthly paradise. There was no sickness, no evil, no death, and God freely roamed in the Garden and communed with them. They wanted for nothing and all was bliss, except for one small catch: God created human beings with the ability to make choices, including to love God in return, or not. And that, ultimately, was their downfall. God tested that love through their willingness to obey His rules for the Garden. When God told Adam and Eve that they could eat from any tree except the Tree of Knowledge of Good and Evil, they chose to eat from it anyway.

Evil, as the story goes, was thereby unleashed upon an otherwise perfect world. It infiltrated the Garden, Adam and Eve, and the earth's bone and marrow. Their disobedience led to the corruption of mankind and eating from that tree opened the eyes of Adam and Eve to evil. They would never experience innocence again. The Tree of Knowledge became more alluring to the eye, but underneath the flesh of its plump fruit and its meaty bark, it became deadly poison. Not poison to the body, but poison to the soul. When God discovered what Adam and Eve had done, He abandoned the Garden forever, and banished them from Eden.

Most who hear the Genesis narrative, as well as those who tell it, do not realize that this is not the end of the story. There are sections that never made it into the Hebrew Bible, or any other version of the creation narrative. At some point they were written down, and copied, but the written copies were few. For most of those who are familiar with missing pieces they were largely passed down by word of mouth over the course of millennia. There is a group of adherents to these writings, and although they do not dispute the Hebrew Bible or any other version of the creation story, for this group it is the collection of missing writings and the unique knowledge found in them that wields real power.

The question naturally arises: what do these writings, also known by the same Sumerian root word Zidug, teach? Though it is impossible to get a hold of a copy of an intact Zidug, the teachings are zealously consistent. With respect to the Genesis narrative and the fall of the human race via that fateful act of disobedience, this is what we find. The Hebrew version is correct: Adam and Eve were banished from the Garden, and left Eden for good after they disobeyed God. They settled in a new land and Eve gave birth to many sons and daughters, but we are only made familiar with three of them: Cain and Abel, and later Seth. Cain was a farmer, and Abel a shepherd. Cain, in a fit of jealous rage, kills his brother Abel and then lies to God about it. He was therefore banished to a land called Nod east of Eden, and although he was a farmer he was cursed to never till the land again.

It is here that the Zidug carries the story on its own. There are many theories based on loose references to Cain about what happened to him after that fateful incident. But this is what really happened, as written in the Zidug: In fact Cain, once banished, does leave and move to Nod with his wife Awan. But they do not stay there. Cain is obsessed with rediscovering Eden. He believes that if he can find the Garden the soil is so rich nothing will be able to stop him from farming again. He only knows Eden from the otherworldly descriptions shared with him by his banished and pining parents since he was a child, but from the moment he leaves Nod, finding Eden becomes his singular focus. His search is long and exasperating, going off vague descriptions and memories shared with him as a boy that often led nowhere. But Cain is nothing if not relentless, and after twenty long years of searching, he is finally successful. Coming over the hill of what appears to be an endless desert, he rounds a small mountain which is uncharacteristically green and lush on its backside given the desert landscape of the region. As he continues to round the mountain, extended family in tow, the vegetation becomes thicker, greener, more vital. And then there it was. Cain stood with Awan on a precipice looking down into a valley unlike anything he had seen before: Eden.

Every possible fruit on the face of the planet, every flower, streams of water that looked like bubbling brooks of liquid honey. It was like stumbling upon heaven on earth, where animals and birds roamed freely, and in Eden, death did not come, sickness did not plague. Cain looking out on what was before him fell on his knees and wept for joy.

Though they did not realize it, the beauty of the Garden was only a mask covering its underlying decay. It turns out that the Garden, though it still appeared in all its beauty and lush glory, was deeply tainted. In the DNA and marrow of the plants and sentient life that continued to grow unabated there, a profound and pernicious corruption thrived there. It was undetectable to the human eye, yet rampant, and it took hold of anything that lived there. The source was the tree, the very tree that ushered evil into the world, the Tree of the Knowledge of Good and Evil. It towered over the center of the Garden and had grown for decades unabated, its roots and seed flooding the Garden. All the animals ate of it, and its fruit was the first thing Cain ate upon his descent into the Garden oasis. They all ate it, that day and every day thereafter.

Cain took up his residency in Eden with Awan and their children, and they continued to grow their community there. They had countless children and grandchildren, generation upon generation lived in that garden. They all ate of the Tree of Knowledge and bit by bit their bodies, minds and souls were irrevocably altered. Eating one piece of fruit from that tree was sufficient to launch evil onto the world and to bring suffering and damnation on the entire human race. The daily consumption from that tree, unabated over time, did far worse to those unaware souls who made their home there. They slowly transformed into mere shadows of human life, eventually consumed by evil, yet none the wiser. Even Satan is believed to know the difference between good and evil and to choose evil. Cain and his descendants eventually became incapable of distinguishing between the two.

And so they carried on, unable to leave the Garden because the fruit of the Tree began to sustain and hold them, while descending deeper and deeper into hopeless degeneration. That's not to say the growth of the Garden was interrupted, if anything it was accelerated, almost as if it was a malignant cancer. Yet the cancer could not be detected by outward appearance. The community of Cain eventually destroyed itself, with the exception of a group who took it upon themselves to leave and start their own community. They took with them saplings of the Tree to plant in their new home, so they could replenish the vast reserves they brought with them for the journey. And thus, the Tree began to spread across the world.

This new group of Cain's diaspora grew plentiful and vast. To anyone encountering one of these descendants, at first they would be none the wiser, but over time it would become clear that these individuals were missing something profound. The first clue would be in their eyes, a lack of life or sparkle, just dullness, but also in the way they viewed life, how they treated others, and their complete lack of concern for right and wrong. They had no interest in distinguishing between the two because the fruit and its seed, over decades, centuries and millennia, robbed them of their souls. This new community at some point became known as the Ziduga, from the same root as the text, and they largely kept to themselves. They did not advertise their existence, and they still do not, but they are everywhere in our world, in every country, city, town. They are our neighbors and co-workers, though they will not divulge their identity.

Some Ziduga are more active than others, active at wreaking chaos and destruction in the world around them, but all of them seek to destroy life in one way or another. Some are geniuses and use their intellectual capabilities to perform unbelievably sinister forms of evil. Others, less intelligent, and they simply carry out their mission violently. Occasionally, they will experience a conflict. It is rare, but it does happen, that the good that also exists in the universe, will seek its day in the sun, and for brief moments in time, some remnant of conscience will rear its head, but it never lasts long before it is relegated back to the bowels of their being. They all hear the Voice, and it plagues them from a young age until death takes them home. All resist the Voice at first, but eventually succumb. They have no choice, because it is relentless and debilitating. The Ziduga must do what it says or they will not be able to function.

The half-breeds are the most cursed of all. They are half-souls, in constant torment because they are violently pulled toward evil, yet have a conscience that fights this inexorable pull. They hear the Voice, yet also hear the voice of conscience. It's extremely rare that a Ziduga would mate with a non-Ziduga, but when it does happen the offspring of this unholy union are borne into the worst of hells. Most go insane, shut down their minds completely, or kill themselves at a young age. Very few survive this torment long.

And so, what does this have to do with our current tale? Though all descendants of Cain, the Ziduga today do not come from any single country, ethnicity or social status. They can be found anywhere in the world, yet most of us will never know of their existence because of their nearly perfect record of keeping their identity a secret. It just so happened that Howard's now-deceased parents, Mark and Lissa, were both descendants of Cain and therefore Ziduga. Just look at the seemingly violent and senseless trajectory of their lives for more than enough supportive evidence. And the same can be said of their predecessors who brought the knowledge of their inheritance to them, as well as

Howard who received it from them. It was to this inheritance and their faith that Howard's life was fully dedicated before he could speak. Incidentally, the adoptive, elderly Louisa Sandground, who was biologically unrelated to Howard and unaware of his lineage, wholeheartedly believed she could provide a fresh start for Howard by passing as his biological grandmother after the death of his parents. She was wrong.

Mark and Lissa met each other as adolescents at a state foster home in New Mexico. Both were left for dead by their parents. From the moment they met they made it their mission to work together to do what they could to wreak destruction on the world. They left the home together by sneaking off in the middle of the night when both were thirteen. As a symbolic sealing of their commitment, they made their way to Europe by stowing away on a cargo ship, then from Europe traveled by land into the Middle East. They snuck across the border into Iraq and made their own attempt to find Eden, but after a year of searching were unsuccessful. All the Ziduga know this history of Cain and Eden because they have heard the words of the Zidug spoken to them. For most they receive the oral tradition. A rare few hold these words in written copy.

Mark and Lissa were one couple that held a partial copy of the Zidug, and they knew every word of it, but the clues found in the text were insufficient to lead them back to Eden. There are

Zidug in recent history rumored to have successfully located the Garden, but it is impossible to know for sure. We just know that Mark and Lissa did not. So they returned to New Mexico and not long thereafter Lissa gave birth to Howard. (Howard was their second attempt. Their first child was stillborn.) Both Mark and Lissa committed him to the same fate as theirs, to live a life faithful to the Zidug and the dictates of the Voice, though the fate was his regardless.

The Garden may be lost forever, but the Tree is not. As mentioned earlier, the seed of its fruit have been taken outside of the Garden and planted. For a reason still unknown, the seeds will only sprout, root and grow in very particular soils in only a few parts of the world. As one might imagine, those locations are known only by the Zidug and guarded very carefully. They also guard the fruit with their lives because they need it themselves. Their souls, or what used to be their souls, crave it viciously, and they store it up for to ensure there is always a supply available to them. It is impossible to estimate how many Ziduga exist in the world as most are unknown and meticulous about masking their identity, the "Mask of Cain." They must conceal their identities because they are born with the belief that they have a mission on this earth, and nothing can be allowed to stop them from fulfilling it. So, they do walk amongst us, but they are Masked so they can continue to perform their mission largely unencumbered.

Some have a brief mission, some a long one. None reveal who they are or the reason for their behavior. Hence, over the centuries and millennia, the world around them has been left dumbfounded by the sheer intensity and utter depravity of their acts without any logical explanation. In the end though, the explanation is logical enough: they are Ziduga.

Those extremely rare few who are not descendants of Cain but somehow uncover knowledge of the Ziduga do their very best to keep it to themselves. There's a good reason for this: Ziduga will destroy not only anyone or anything that threatens to stop them from fulfilling their mission, but also anyone or anything that threatens to reveal them. So those who are aware do not share this knowledge with anyone else. And if they do, they will go to extremes to ensure it goes no further.

C HAPTER 20.
THE GATHERING

Bubby did not go to churches often. As a non-practicing Jewish woman, she didn't go to synagogues much either. She didn't have anything against either of them, but there wasn't any reason to go. She figured that when she wanted to speak to God, she could do it just as easily from the comfort of her own home. And certainly, God could hear her no matter where she was, so it shouldn't matter to Him either.

But there was a good reason for her to be at church today, albeit for the first time in a long time. She wasn't the most mobile person in the world, but she was sharp as a whip and refused to give up her driver's license, so she drove there that evening. Parking in the back of the church, she saw two other cars there, both of which she recognized. That was a relief. It was a Thursday night just before 9:00 pm.

She got out of the car and started making her way up the walkway to the rear door. The church appeared dark inside, at least in the hallways and outer windows. There wasn't a sign of anyone inside, though she knew better. She pulled on the handle and the door opened. She vaguely remembered the way to the room they had met in several times before and made her way there. She could hear muffled voices inside and light coming from under the door in the otherwise dark church. To her surprise the door opened just as she was reaching for the handle. Pastor Tom, surprised and pleased to see her standing there, welcomed her with a hug.

"Belsa, it's been too long. So good to see you."

"Tom. Villiam." She leaned forward to see William Mittford already seated inside.

"Hi Belsa. Good to see you." William acknowledged her as well as he stood up.

Pastor Tom opened the door and motioned for her to enter the windowless choir practice room. Cream robes with maroon trim hung on rods along the walls arranged by size. There were three folding chairs arranged in a circle in the middle of the room. Other than that, the décor was unremarkable.

"Please have a seat Belsa." Tom motioned toward the closest chair. "I'll be back in a minute."

William Mittford, a scholarly-looking man in his early to mid-fifties, well dressed and well groomed, sat down as well.

"How long has it been Belsa. Must be at least two years, no?"

"At least." Belsa nodded. "Zings have been quiet recently. Ve knew it must end someday."

"Indeed. Indeed." Will agreed as he thought about the implications of her words.

William Mittford looked scholarly, probably because he was. He was a professor at the university about one hundred miles north, which was where he lived. He taught archaeology and history, which is what he had done his entire professional life. That's all he ever wanted to do. His doctoral thesis was written on the lost Sumerian civilization of the ancient near east, and although all his brilliant work was done at Ivy League universities, including his doctoral thesis at the University of Pennsylvania's Department of Archaeology, he had no interest in teaching there despite a very enticing offer. As soon as he finished his studies he returned to his home town and had been there ever since.

"The doors are now locked." Pastor Tom reentered the room and shut the door behind them. "So, Will and Belsa, thank you both for making the trek over here. And Will, I'm curious why the urgent call for a meeting?"

"Sure, right. Well, thank you for hosting. So, I know it's been a long time since we've met together. If I am calculating correctly, it was just over three years ago. At that time, fortunately, there wasn't much for us to discuss as things were pretty quiet. But that has changed." He glanced at Belsa and Tom before continuing.

"There is something stirring amongst the *community*." He emphasized community for effect.

Tom and Belsa knew exactly what he meant.

"What makes you think that, Will?"

"Tom, he is right," Belsa affirmed. "I sense it as vell."

"Well, as you know Tom, I've been studying the community and its history for many years now. Most of my life, actually." Looking at the floor he collected his thoughts. "Throughout the history of the Ziduga," he whispered the last word, "there have been intermittent periods of, let's say...nervous energy."

"Vat is nervous energy? Ju mean ven they start impacting ze vorld in significant vays?"

"Yes, yes. There seem to be cycles of activity, small bursts of activity separated by decades, but then substantial transformative upheavals, let's say, every few hundred years or so. What's strange this time is that this one comes pretty closely on the heels of a previous major episode."

"Ju mean Vorld Var II."

"Yes, exactly. That was relatively recent history, which means if I am correct, the current developments are a significant anomaly."

"But what developments are you referring to, Will? I haven't detected anything out of the ordinary. Belsa, you said you've been seeing things as well?"

"Jes, zere is definitely movement. Somezing is coming. I feel a profound turmoil, and I have felt it for a long time now."

She thought about it, then added, "I really

didn't vant to believe it, so I ignored it. But jes, jes, it is definitely very powerful at ze moment."

"Yes, Tom, something major is taking place. I'm not sure exactly what, but they have been getting progressively more active over the last few years or so. Perhaps longer, but about a year and a half ago was when I started to detect something going on and started paying attention. Their actions have been more destructive and coordinated. I'm convinced of it."

"But what do you think is behind it?"

Belsa answered the question for him: "For evil to vin."

The simplicity and the profundity of that statement left them all momentarily speechless.

"Hmmm. Ok, I believe you. I haven't felt it myself, but that doesn't mean anything. So, what do you think we should do about it? Or, I guess, a better question is, is there anything we can do about it?"

"Jes. There is."

"What's that Belsa?" Tom and Will both looked at her.

"History is coming full circle. Ve must unify and destroy zem, before zey destroy us."

Tom didn't expect that.

"Destroy us? Destroy who?"

"History has alvays been moving in zis direction. From ze beginning, ze goal vas to destroy creation."

"She's actually right, Tom, there have been

markers pointing to this for quite some time now."

"Ve all know about zis race. Zer is something far more sinister mobilizing them and it vas never satisfied vith anything less zan ze end of creation itself. I have felt it for some time now. Everyzing is coming to a climax."

"I do agree with her, Tom. I think this is why the cycles are accelerating."

"Well, as you both know, I believe that God ultimately wins here. But from my reading of Revelation, there is a lot of pain and suffering that happens in the process. I don't know if there's any way to change that, but I do agree that we need to do something. I'm just not sure what."

"Tom, I vish I had jour conviction about who God is. But alas, I don't. I do, believe zere is a God. Zat's been enough for me. At zis point, ve all need to ask God for help."

Will stood up and began to pace the room. "So Belsa, when you say 'unify and destroy them' what exactly do you mean?"

Belsa reflected for a moment. "Vill, ze biggest advantage ze Ziduga have has alvays been zeir anonymity. Vith ze exception of a few, and ve don't know how many zat is, ze human race has been ignorant of zeir existence. Ve need to change zat."

Will stopped pacing and faced her. "Belsa, you know that means certain death for us. Jim didn't even get that far and he disappeared."

"Jim vasn't very smart about it."

Jim was a cautionary tale for anyone considering a confrontation with the Ziduga community. He was the one who most strongly believed that exposure was the way to fight back against the Ziduga, or at the very least to contain them. His belief was that they would only get one chance to do it, so they needed to go big, and for the US they agreed that probably meant the *New York Times*. Jim wrote the article, which was over twenty pages long, and included absolutely everything they knew about the cursed race. The group all had copies and agreed that it was the right thing to do. They disagreed on the execution though. Tom, Will and Belsa were adamant that Jim mail the article anonymously, but he didn't think anyone would take it seriously. He insisted on going himself. They agreed to sleep on it and reconvene the next day to make a final decision, but Jim had already made his mind up.

That night he made himself a small travel bag and started the drive to New York. He drove straight through, and the next day he called Tom from Manhattan as soon as he got there. He apologized for his unilateral decision, but he stood by his belief that it was the only way. That was the last they heard from him. He never called again and he never came back. Perhaps out of their respect for Jim, or a last-ditch attempt at hope, they continued to check the *Times* every day for months, but the article was never published.

Tom finally broke the silence. "Yes, Belsa,

you're right about that."

Will started pacing again. "The fact is they're everywhere, so you never know when you're being eyed."

"I try not to think about it. The paranoia used to drive me insane."

"Vell, I'm fortunate. I've already tasted death and survived so it doesn't scare me. Besides, I'm not going to be around on zis earth much longer, so I'm villing to take ze risk."

"None of us knows how much time we have, Belsa," Tom said solemnly. "So how do the two of you propose we take away their advantage?"

They were startled by a knock at the door. All three of them froze.

After waiting in silence for another knock, Tom finally responded, "Who is it?" There was no answer. Tom asked again as he moved closer to the door. Again, no response. He cracked the door and seeing no one there he poked his head out into the darkness.

"Oh, Tom!" they heard a woman call from down the hallway.

"Oh, hi there Esther." Tom stepped out and closed the door behind him. They could make out bits and pieces of the muffled conversation in the hallway.

"Yes, yes. Ok, we're just finishing up some church business. Thank you, Esther."

He reentered with a clear expression of relief. "Esther's the cleaning lady. I forgot she comes tonight."

They were all visibly relieved.

"Perhaps we should take a break, Tom. Grab a bite to eat?"

"Great idea. We can resume our conversation at a later time."

"But ve mustn't vait long. Time is of ze essence."

They all agreed and left the church for the evening.

C HAPTER 21. DEADENING

There comes a time in everyone's life, or in most people's lives, when they realize that they are only a very small piece in a vast cosmic puzzle. That their lives are, in fact, inconsequential. The qualification of "most people" is necessary because there are exceptions to this rule, and Howard was one of them. Howard was uniquely disinterested in seeing the larger perspective or in trying to see what role he played, if any, in the world. He did seem to have some appreciation for the fact that he was not in control of his circumstances and that something else was in charge. It's quite possible that to him that meant nothing more than the Voice. But regardless, he knew at a young age there were some things he had no control over and he left it at that.

If Howard ever studied philosophy, which he did not, he probably would have appreciated Thomas Hobbes more than most. Though with a few modifications. Howard was attracted to evil because that's what he believed he was put on earth to do. There was no guilt or selfishness underlying his actions; to him that's simply the way it was. He was fully aware of his ancestry and the tribe he came from. He didn't blame his lineage or consider genes the cause of his behavior. Both were simply statements of fact. Causation was not relevant.

Howard also recognized that most others on the planet did not live this way and that was fine. Whether others realized it or not, the world was a hostile, anarchic environment, and life was nasty, brutish and short. He believed that was the reason they believed in God, because otherwise the grim reality was too much to bear. God was something man contrived to help ease the pain; something made up to make sense of the nonsense. His parents told him this almost daily. His adoptive grandmother lived in a completely different paradigm. Either way, it didn't matter.

The irony was, and Howard was still too young to understand this when his parents died, his parents to all appearances did have a god in the sense that they had a reason for living. They heard the Voice as well, which fueled them onward, kept them fighting. Their mission was to destroy, to create chaos, to engage in acts of cruelty for cruelty's sake. But that was the real irony: if you gave the record of these two people's lives even a cursory look, the negligent abuse of their son, the reckless destruction for the sake of being destructive, the robbing of life from countless individuals...all of these things just on the face of them, seemed driven by a mission. In fact, they were, and they had committed their lives to it. And this only began to come into focus after they were dead, because they were as effective as Howard at avoiding either being implicated or caught. In fact, their whole race seemed to have that same eerie, elusive quality.

And here's the bigger irony: they also knew, as did everyone in the Ziduga community, that there was something in opposition to the Voice. They simply had committed their lives to the power of the Voice instead. They didn't believe they had a choice, and they didn't think about whether they had a choice. Their commitment to that power behind the Voice, whatever it was, was so consuming that the idea that there was anything else competing for their devotion seemed beyond their grasp. So they released it.

After Howard's parents died, and some of the evidence of their criminal involvement started to fit together, there were a few local news stories about the couple. But the full extent of their activities was never fully uncovered, and the story never went any further. The conclusion that the local community came to was one that fit their understanding of the universe: they were good people gone horrifically bad, negligent parents that had been abandoned themselves. And as for Howard, he had the good fortune of a loving adoptive home. Initially it was believed that in the hands of his adoptive grandmother figure, Howard was young and malleable enough that his behavior would correct itself. With his parents gone all would now be well.

There was one individual in particular, a Dr. Siderow who taught at the local community college, who took a special interest in Howard and the story of his parents. He was a professor of religion and religious history. He tried to speak with Howard's parents several times before they died, though they never accepted his invitation. Dr. Siderow did his PhD on the history of religious texts and their influence on church history, and he was well respected in the field. He was also an acquaintance of William Mittford, though he was not fully aware of the Ziduga as Will Mittford was. He did, however, have his suspicions.

Dr. Siderow was interviewed in a PBS documentary many years ago on the subject of religious texts, making him one of the few who approached celebrity status in the town. At that time he had acolytes across religious faiths, primarily the faiths of the Book, meaning Judaism, Christianity and Islam, though popular opinion quickly turned against him.

On the PBS feature he explored the genesis of the ancient, doctrinal texts, and how some evolved into religious canon, while others fell by the wayside. The Bible, for example was canonized by the Catholic Church at the Council of Nicaea. Similarly, Judeo and Muslim religious leaders granted doctrinal authority to the Torah and the

Quran. If he had stopped there, there probably wouldn't have been any issue. But about a year and a half after the special Dr. Siderow started making claims that upset the wrong people. He couldn't provide any empirical evidence to support it, but he insisted that there were other texts in existence that were suppressed for centuries by the Judeo-Christian authorities and that those texts contradicted some of what was accepted church history.

It was about this same time that Dr. Siderow was in a deadly car accident. The other driver was killed on impact, but Dr. Siderow, also being the sole person in his car, survived. He emerged physically unscathed except for a severe concussion and a permanent brain injury. The injury didn't damage his intelligence or his cognitive faculties, but it did affect his speech: he was left with a stutter that became debilitating when he spoke in public.

After he had recovered from the accident, he did resume touring and speaking, but the stutter, particularly when he was questioned about his findings regarding the unsubstantiated texts, would become so pronounced that it left the listener with the distinct impression that he was not being forthright, and that he didn't believe what he was saying. On top of this unfortunate set of circumstances, there were rumors that he was high on pills when the accident occurred, though that was never proven.

The end result was that he was less and less

sought after as an authority on these matters, and ultimately disappeared from the speaking circuit altogether.

The irony is that his claims were, in fact, correct.

As Dr. Siderow lost opportunities to speak publicly, he turned his attention to writing. He published a book, under Yale University Press, that outlined his philosophy of humanistic meaning. His writings became angrier and angrier, him claiming that the church used religious texts as a means to political power, not a source of truth. He was on a relentless quest to substantiate his claims regarding the additional texts, but he was ultimately unsuccessful. He died a couple of years later of a heart attack in his kitchen. He lived alone and they didn't find him until several days later. There was some controversy there as well. There were those who claimed that Dr. Siderow was poisoned and that the poison triggered the heart attack. Dr. Siderow had plenty of detractors and it wasn't considered unlikely, though the coroner's report was inconclusive.

Tripp found a copy of the tape as he was rummaging through a living room cabinet and inserted it in. Tripp's parents had made a copy of the PBS special when it aired because it was rare enough for a local to appear on national television that it warranted taping. The special was interesting to Tripp, but more interesting were some of the shorter interviews that followed it on the same tape. In those, there were references to additional texts that made a connection for Tripp. He had never seen Howard's book unwrapped, but he knew about it and he had an idea of what it meant to Howard.

Dr. Siderow stubbornly defended his point of view, which again didn't help his cause. He argued that the source of all the world's ills could be reduced to religious belief and the texts upon which those beliefs were built. And the reason was not that they were not true, but because they were incomplete. We didn't have the full picture that God, whichever manifestation of God you choose to believe in, wanted us to have. And so each religious faith would try to support their version and suppress the rest, known and unknown. The manifestation of these disputes were wars, pogroms, colonialism, slavery, but the philosophical, or theological underpinnings for the actions were entirely different and based on an incomplete understanding of the truth.

Dr. Siderow spoke quite frequently on these matters on television prior to the accident, and his book was devoted to it later on. There was a group that supported his views and worked with him to assimilate the texts, including what they believed were contained in the undiscovered ones, into one coherent whole. But the additional ones were not found, and interest in creating a universal religious text was minimal outside of this group.

The movement didn't gain much momentum, not just because the texts could never be proven, but also because of the efforts of established religions to undermine it. The movement started in Egypt, and spread widely, albeit thinly, throughout the Middle East, then to parts of the rest of the world. The start of a universal text was developed by the small but tenacious group at the heart of the movement. They felt it was critical to continue moving forward, but they were always looking over their shoulders and did their work in secrecy.

Their concerns were well-founded. The Roman church, in particular, was aggressive in tracking the followers of this still fledgling faith and trying to shut them down. So were the scholarly authorities of the Muslim faith. Members of the group started to disappear without any trace, and once the persecution started in earnest, any copies of the seminal book that were found were destroyed. It is widely believed that someone had obtained copies of the additional texts that had been incorporated in this new universal text, and that a portion of the additional text was from the Zidug. Furthermore, it may have been authorities of the Christian and Muslim faiths in name who were pursuing these individuals, but there can be no doubt that the ones who were most aggressive were the Ziduga, whatever priestly attire they were wearing.

In the end, those left of the group tried their best to make as many copies of their integrated text as possible and hide them. But those integrated texts were either lost or destroyed, and no one outside this group, which essentially disappeared, had a copy. None of the source texts, were ever produced either.

The book Howard carried around with him, despite appearances, was not a source text. Though Howard acted as though he was carrying a partial copy of the Zidug, which he would carefully wrap and hide away, it was not. It was part of his plan, developed early on, to protect the text at all costs. He knew that if he carried the book on his person, it would only be a matter of time before it was taken from him and destroyed. The original was hidden. Well-hidden. The book he carried with him was a decoy, and perhaps for lack of anything else of value in his life, he always carried it close to him and treated it as if it were sacred itself. He knew full well, however, that the actual text, the text that carried the ancient words of his race, was buried where no one would even think to look. Howard had put the book in a wooden box he had built with his own hands, and placed the box into the palms of his father's cold, dead hands the day he was buried. The handful of people that attended the funeral probably assumed he was placing memories of his childhood with his father.

The interesting thing is that no connection was made in Dr. Siderow's interviews with Howard or Howard's parents and the ideas that he was promoting. The fact is, Dr. Siderow suspected a lot more than he let on in his interviews and his books. He suspected a race rooted in the history of the Ziduga, though he did not identify them as such. He also suspected, and this was a real mystery as to how or why, that Howard's parents were a part of this race. He did not, however, know that Howard's father had part of an authentic copy of the text.

So about as far as he got was the history of the sacred books and the movement that produced them. He would have loved to get his hands on one, to finally put to rest the nagging skepticism that he had to suppress throughout his later years as he never actually came up with the proof he desperately sought.

This he could never quite shake off, but only suppress, because not only had he not seen any of the source books, but no one he knew had physically seen them either, in spite of claims to the contrary. Those texts remained vexingly elusive. There was one individual that he met at a conference, Jonathan Bix, who used to work at the Metropolitan Museum of Art in New York City, where he curated their ancient manuscript collection for six years. He claimed to have seen a genuine copy of one of the ancient books in question. He claimed to have seen it when a French atheist philosopher, Jean Thierault, was doing a book tour of his most recent work in the United States and shared it with him in secrecy. But even this whole story was called into question by a colleague of Mr. Bix at the Museum, Quentin Sayville. Quentin claimed he had it on good authority that the book never existed and was a ruse to manipulate Jonathan Bix. In the end, the two men ended up having a love affair, and are believed to have died in a crash, along with the pilot and co-pilot, when their plane inexplicably disappeared en route to the British Virgin Islands. Neither the plane nor the bodies have been recovered to date, and this promising lead eventually came to another strange and wholly unsatisfying conclusion for Dr. Siderow.

The long and short of it is this: Dr. Siderow found after countless false starts and empty promises that evidence of any of these books and their contents was virtually impossible to find. Everyone who claimed to be in possession of one of the books, and apart from Jean Thierault he knew of only two others, were very secretive about their possessions and they almost never discussed it in public.

Not long after the deaths of Jonathan Bix and Jean Thierault, something started to occur that Dr. Siderow described in his book as the awakening of a "sleeper cell". He claimed that a movement was beginning to take shape that had its roots in the ancient soil of time and space. He described it as something cosmic in nature, like a supernatural hand moving the pieces of a giant jigsaw puzzle that was starting to take shape. He believed that he himself was one of those pieces.

This was some time after his book was published, and by this time, most thought that Dr. Siderow damaged a lot more than his speech in his car accident. At the end, very few considered him as more than an eccentric crackpot.

Though it would be a stretch to label Dr. Siderow a conventional theist, he did believe in forces at work in the universe and that religious texts contained the voices of those forces. He also remained convinced, until his dying breath, that there were hidden texts out there that had been suppressed. Despite the nagging itch of skepticism that gnawed at the back of his mind, in spite of the loss of reputation, esteem, recognition and income, he never let that belief go. In some of the quieter moments of loneliness or self-doubt, deep misgivings would rear their ugly heads and suggest to him that perhaps he had made a big mistake. Perhaps his life's work, the convictions he lived and would ultimately die for, his life's passion to free people from the shackles of ignorance and to open their minds to the whole truth, not the carefully spliced and manicured truth they were fed by their religious mentors, perhaps all of this was actually a mistake. Maybe his own convictions were the wrong ones, and maybe there really wasn't more out there than what had been in their hands for thousands of years. Maybe he had committed his life to a huge mistake, a misguided falsehood, and maybe he should cut his losses, return to the church of his youth, and stop pursuing these phantom writings. Maybe the hell he learned of in Sunday School as a boy was preparing a seat at the fire because of his stubbornness. If so, his eternity would not be a pleasant one. And it wasn't only the fear of eternal damnation that in those rare, still moments jarred him, but perhaps worse was the glimpse of how insignificant his life on this side of death would be if he had spent it chasing a lie.

But then he always came back to what he knew. That despite a seeming lack of intention behind the circumstances now unfolding, there were things happening leading toward a clear conclusion. He couldn't put his finger on what that conclusion was or what it meant, but he knew that it was there, and in his better moments he knew it beyond a shadow of a doubt. He had no choice but to simply go along for the ride, and he also believed that whatever questions remained, they would eventually be answered, whether by him or someone else. This meant eventually getting hold of the texts themselves and presenting them publicly for all the world to see. Then, all the world would know the truth and he would be vindicated.

An interesting sidenote about Dr. Siderow. His precipitous fall from grace, and the resultant manifestation of that in terms of his speech impairment, his loss of income and some stress-related health issues, made no difference in terms of how he conducted himself. He lost his position as a professor shortly after his speaking engagements dried up. His books also sold poorly. But in spite of his circumstances, he didn't take it out on the world around him. He treated others, particularly strangers, with respect and kindness. Dr. Siderow was one of the most ethical and honest men one could meet. At his very core, he was a man of conviction. Aggrieved, yes, but a defender of truth at any cost. And that is what led him to stand by the convictions he believed to be accurate, despite the pain it caused him and the horrible circumstances into which this conviction drove his life.

That is not to say that he didn't have his enemies, foremost of whom was James Sasser. Sasser was an ordained minister in the Baptist church, and he came from a long line of ministers. He loved being a minister, and he loved his flock. He relished every bit of his role. His flock returned the favor and couldn't speak highly enough of their "Pastor James". Pastor James went above and beyond the call of duty, making it his mission to serve every member of his congregation to the utmost of his ability and then some. But Pastor James nursed a secret that he did not share with his congregation or even his closest friends and confidantes. When he was young, he lost his parents in a car accident that he was a witness to. He was a passenger in the car and saw his parents crushed to death before his very eyes by a tractor trailer truck that ran red light and hit the family car head on. The impact of the fully loaded truck, traveling at an estimated 50 miles per hour, demolished the front half of the car where his mother and father were sitting. Miraculously, the impact Jimmy with a couple of broken bones and plenty of scrapes, but nothing more serious. When it was all over, he sat buckled into the back seat of a car flipped on its side, several feet from both of his parents, dead, and all of them entombed in a case of twisted metal and plastic.

For many, at this tender young age, this would have been an open and shut case for either atheism or an enduring hatred of any sort of God or higher power. For Pastor Jimmy, it led to a life of devotion to God. He somehow internalized this life-altering event as the turning point of his life. As a boy, he had always harbored a secret fear that his parents would abandon him if he wasn't good enough, and he lived, even at this young age, with a constant, gnawing suspicion that he wasn't. In the dark recesses of his mind, this fear and his parents' death were connected. So now little James was paralyzed with fear at the prospect of being parentless at the age of eight, and he immediately latched on to God to assuage this fear. He no longer had an earthly father, so he would now commit his life to serving his heavenly father, and he began his steady march toward the church. He wanted to keep this new father happy, and he went to great lengths to please him, out of a deep-seated dread that his new father might also leave him if he disappointed him. The surest way to prevent that from happening was to commit his life to serving

Him full time by joining the ministry. Indeed, that was the result.

Years later, Sasser also saw the Siderow documentary on PBS. His revulsion with Siderow, and everything he stood for, hatched there and grew. He was convinced that Dr. Siderow was an over-educated, unprincipled, ivory tower type without any meaningful convictions to guide him in life. James Sasser took it as a personal affront that anyone would try to create mythical texts, that clearly didn't exist, and that the goal was nothing more than to delegitimize the texts that were true, like the Bible, and which formed the foundation of everything he stood for in life. Pastor James didn't get angry about too many things, but this was the one thing that made him livid. That meant Dr. Siderow was the target, and Pastor James became his most vocal critic. He took the initiative to track his appearances and commentary and made sure there was always a resounding repudiation present or in the works. What made it worse, in James Sasser's eyes, is that he didn't think Dr. Siderow believed what he was defending. He thought that he was simply doing it for publicity. The irony is that both men were driven by the same thing: their integrity and their convictions.

Dr. Siderow, for his part, found the flurry of activity coming from James Sasser troubling at first, more because he didn't like his integrity being called into question than anything else. But as Dr. Siderow's reputation declined, Sasser's grew.

Ultimately, for all the reasons cited above, Siderow was left with no audience at all. Pastor Sasser claimed that he had won, or rather that God had claimed the victory, and that an evil had been defeated.

When Dr. Siderow was found dead at his kitchen table several months later, and just a few weeks after his heart attack, Pastor Sasser was immediately considered a prime suspect. Fortunately for Sasser, he was visiting family out of state at the time. After a lengthy investigation, it was determined that there was no foul play, at least not at the hands of James Sasser.

C HAPTER 22. COUNTDOWN

"If I had a dime for every time you said that..." Officer Wagner didn't complete his thought.

"Yeah?" his longtime partner Detective Lindsay beckoned from behind his computer screen without looking up. "Well, finish your thought."

"You know. I'd be a rich man."

Lindsay stopped typing. "Look, all I'm saying is that we'll eventually get our man. But even so, there will be ten more to replace him."

Wagner looked over his computer monitor at him. "I think you're getting close to retirement. You won't have to worry about that much longer." He smiled wryly and started searching for something in his desk drawer.

Lindsay sat up in his vinyl chair and took another sip of lukewarm coffee out of the Styrofoam cup. He was about to reply, but then forgot what he was going to say. They had spent since the wee hours of the morning trying to comb through the evidence of another murder in their county.

This one didn't follow the pattern of the prior three that occurred elsewhere in the state, which troubled them both. But there enough similarities that they believed it was a copycat. A careless one. This one appeared to have been perpetrated by someone less skilled, so chances were he left a trace somewhere. Lindsay took another sip, then finished the rest, crumpled the cup and threw it away as he slouched in his chair again.

"You know Tom, you may be right."

Wagner looked aside from his screen again and eyed him. "About what?" He had completely lost track of their original conversation, now focused on trying to find the birthday gift he had bought for his wife weeks before.

Jim Lindsay just stared out the window.

Wagner returned to his rummaging and asked again. "You know I'm always right, Jim, but what are you referring to?"

After a long pause, the detective refocused and responded that he meant the idea of retirement. "I mean, it's not like I don't think of doing something different. Or just taking time off and driving with Lois across the country." His thoughts drifted to their broken-down RV.

"Of course, Jim, who doesn't? I mean, this job takes a toll on you after a while." He shut the top drawer and started on the middle one. "I think we all think about it at times. But hell, when I think about it long enough I realize I couldn't really do much else," he said to the stuffed drawer.

It was so overstuffed he decided to give up looking. Pushing back from his desk he stared at Lindsay who was still looking out the window into the sunny afternoon.

"What were you thinking of doing?"

Again, after a long pause, "The RV does sound...." but his sentence was interrupted by a junior officer bursting into the room. "Sir, it looks like we may have found both murderers," he said breathlessly. "We found two men that fit the description in an SRO. Two separate boarders. They need you both over there."

Lindsay and Wagner were both up and heading toward the door before he finished speaking. The three of them jumped into the unmarked car parked in front of the station and headed over with two other police cars toward the building. It was only about a ten-minute drive at full speed.

When they arrived there was already a flurry of activity at the building, which was a run-down SRO in arguably the worst section of the city. The block had been cordoned off with "Police Line--Do Not Cross" yellow tape and three police cars and a van were parked in front of the entrance. The two men in question had been arrested and were handcuffed in the back of the van. The owner of the SRO, a thoroughly tattooed man with large biceps and a shiny, cleanly shaven head had been called in from his home and was having a heated discussion with two officers already at the scene.

Wagner, Lindsay and the two junior officers joined them. Wagner and Lindsay didn't listen long before they realized that the questioning wasn't getting very far. After a couple more
minutes of trying to get information regarding the
suspects from the owner, they left him to try their
luck with the resident manager, while the other
officers remained with the owner.

The two lead officers at the scene believed
the owner, Nick, when he told them he didn't
know anything about the men. He didn't live
on the premises and he didn't manage it either.
His right-hand man, the manager, didn't ask too
many questions when renting out rooms. He, quite
frankly, didn't care where the men came from or
what their business was, as long as they paid the
rent. These two men had paid their rent for the five
days they had been staying there. End of story. The
reason for the suspicion and the call into the police
from the manager was quite simple: the two men
attacked another tenant of the flophouse and beat
him to within an inch of his life. The manager kept
his distance, didn't try to interfere, he just called
the police and called the hospital, which sent an
ambulance to pick up the unconscious victim.
This is the information Nick had received from the
resident manager, and it's all he knew.

When the police first arrived, they searched
the rooms of the two men and found very little in
there, but they did find a wad of single bills and
a collection of three knives, two of which had had

dried blood on them. The bundle had been stashed between the bed and the wall of one of the men's rooms. Those were collected and prepared to be sent to a DNA lab. Even after interviewing other residents and searching the rooms, they found nothing that spoke to a motive behind the beating, the relationship between the three men, or the background of the men involved.

The officers decided to leave off questioning the owner for now, and to bring the two suspects into the station. They left their contact information and took the van back. Lindsay and Wagner stayed a bit longer with the resident manager and tried to get what additional information they could out of him, but it wasn't any more than what the owner already told them. As was common in these types of places, people keep to themselves and don't bother with each other's business. Three other officers stayed and continued to search the rooms for more evidence, but they were clean. None of the officers involved made a connection, but seemingly isolated events like this had seen a marked increase in recent months all over the country.

C HAPTER 23.
THE VISIT

Tripp had to make a decision. We all have moments when we face a critical fork in the road, and we know our lives will look very different if we take a left instead of a right. For Tripp, this was one such juncture. He was lying on the couch this muggy July evening staring at the television, but not watching it. He felt as though he was moving away from Howard and all the chaos surrounding Howard; that they represented a prior chapter in his life and that he was headed in the opposite direction. Not to say that he didn't occasionally get jolted back there, but regardless of temporary reconnections with his past, the trajectory was clearly in the other direction.

He was experiencing just such a reconnection at the moment. He was thinking about Nebraska, where there had been an on-location Breaking News report only moments before. Yet another killing spree, with no clear motive and no leads on the perpetrator. In his head he was traveling through the house in Nebraska where the incident occurred, looking for Howard, looking for something, anything, to make sense of the chaotic mess. He was pulled back into the present by a sudden knock on the door. Tripp sat up, a little scared, as he and his sister were alone in the house. She was upstairs probably in her room and his mother wouldn't be home for a couple of hours. For a moment he wondered if it could be Howard, then he told himself he was just being paranoid. A second knock came, a little louder than the first.

He tried to peek through the front window without being spotted to see who it was, but the front light wasn't on and he couldn't clearly see the man standing there. The television set continued to drone in the background. He made his way to the closed door and asked who it was, trying to make his voice sound a bit deeper and older.

"Hi, my name is Peter O'Neill." There was a brief pause before he continued. "I am looking for a Tripp Talbot. Do I have the right address?"

"What do you need to speak with Tripp about?"

"Ah, yes, well, my understanding is that Tripp had a relationship with a boy named Howard Sandground. I'm a professor at Valley College here in town. I've been doing some research and I wanted to speak with Tripp about Howard."

Tripp could have guessed as much. He paused for a moment, then decided there probably wasn't any harm in speaking with him. He slowly opened the door. "Hi, I'm Tripp," he said in his normal voice.

"Hi Tripp, sorry to bother you. Would your parents be ok with us talking for a minute?"

"Yes, it should be all right." Tripp motioned him into the living room and they sat down.

"Should we invite your parents to join us?"

"No, I think it will be all right. I don't want to bother them right now." Even though his parents were gone he still wanted to hear what the professor had to say.

"Ok, thanks, Tripp. So, you don't know me, but as I said, I'm a professor at the college here and I have a colleague, well had a colleague I should say, named Dr. Siderow."

Tripp thought of the PBS recording.

"I'm not sure if you've heard of Siderow?"

"Yes, I actually found a tape of the PBS special with him on it recently."

"Yes, yes, he was a brilliant man. Well, it's awful what happened to him and as you probably know, he passed away not too long ago."

"Yes, I heard that too."

"Right. So, Dr. Siderow and I spoke quite regularly, even after he left the college. I am quite familiar with his research and we spoke often about Howard and his parents."

Tripp wasn't sure what the connection was, but let him continue.

"I'm aware of your relationship with Howard. I know that you interacted with him a fair bit before he left town." He looked at Tripp to see if there was any reaction. Tripp continued to wonder what the connection was.

"I was wondering..." he paused to consider how to ask the question. "In your interactions with Howard, did he ever mention a book to you? A special book or anything like that?"

Tripp thought for a moment, knowing he had, but still not sure how the pieces fit together.

"Well, yes, I know he had a copy of some book. I never actually saw the book itself. I just know that it was very important to him."

"I see. Yes, I believe that may be a very special book. Did he ever talk about it, or show it to you? I've been doing a fair bit of research in this field, as did Dr. Siderow, and believe that book may have had great historical significance. But I was wondering if you ever actually saw it or what was in it?"

Tripp thought for a moment. "Well, no, I never saw the book itself, but I do know the book you're talking about. Howard had a book wrapped up in a cloth. I mean it looked like a book. But I never saw the book itself. And he never talked about what was in it."

"I see. I know it's strange for me to show up at your house like this. I hope your parents won't be too upset, but I really wanted to speak with you. I also didn't want to call because unfortunately you never know who might be listening."

Tripp was surprised that this information was significant enough to be the subject of a spying operation.

"You should be careful too, Tripp. Especially when you talk about Howard. I believe there may be people watching your house and maybe even you. Not to scare you, but just be aware. It may be the police as they want to see if Howard tries to come to you. I don't know. They're probably listening to your phone calls as well."

Tripp was more surprised to hear this. He didn't think he had any connection worth monitoring, that his connection to Howard had been long forgotten.

He replied with the words his expression already made clear: "I had no idea."

"Well, like I said, they figure this is a prime destination for Howard."

"I haven't seen him or heard from him in a long time. He used to write me, but he hasn't written me in longer than I can remember. I definitely don't think he's coming back here."

"Well, Tripp, you may be right, but they're not going to take any chances. In any event, I came to see you because I wanted to clarify some things."

"Like what?"

"So what you saw with Howard, what he had wrapped up, it may not have been a book at all?"

Tripp thought through this possibility and rejected it. "Well, no, not really. It was definitely a book, and I could tell it had a special meaning to him. He never talked about it with me directly, but I could tell. He didn't own anything, really. He didn't care about things, but he did care about that book. It couldn't be anything else. What kind of book is it anyway? Why is it so important?"

"Well, Tripp..."

"Does it have something to do with all the horrible things he did? A book can't make you commit evil."

"Tripp, people do horrible things for all sorts of reasons, and often without any reason at all. It's not quite that simple. The book didn't make him do anything." He paused. "So, Tripp, I won't get into too many details, and I don't have all the answers, but, let's see, how do I put this..."

Tripp had no doubt that there was something corrupted in Howard, maybe even evil, but he never knew what or why, other than the awful way his parents raised and treated him.

"So, Dr. Siderow was the expert on this, but he shared a lot of his research with me before he passed." He paused again, as if he was struggling to formulate his thoughts. "Tripp, this may sound hard to believe, but there is a race of people on this planet that are different from you and me. I mean, they're human, like us, but they've been corrupted." Another pause.

"You see, Tripp, you and me, we're born with a conscience. We know inside, what's right and what's wrong. We can ignore the voice of our conscience, as many people do, but we have it nonetheless." He leaned forward for emphasis.

"But this race, this sub-race, whatever you want to call it, that voice, their conscience has been all but removed. The distinction between right and wrong does not exist for them."

Tripp was trying to grasp the weight of what he was saying. What would it even look like to not know right from wrong?

"I would actually say it goes a little further than that, Tripp. The fact is, this group not only doesn't care about right and wrong, but they are on a mission to wipe out good on this earth."

All the thoughts and questions swimming around in Tripp's head finally started to overflow. "Who are these people. Where are they? How many are there?"

"That's the difficulty Tripp. No one knows how many, but they are everywhere and they are in our midst. They are all around us, but they are also very good at disguising themselves. Unless you were able to detain one, lock them up in a room and analyze them and their behavior over time, I'm not sure you would even know whether it was a Zid or not."

"A what?"

"A Zid. A Ziduga. They are an ancient race called the Ziduga. They go back to the beginning of the human race. Humankind developed the capacity for what we call conscience or consciousness, self-awareness, but the Ziduga don't have it. I guess the easiest way to describe it is they are a race of people that never developed a soul. They are intelligent and seem normal in probably any other way, but they have no souls."

Tripp was dumbfounded.

"I know this is a lot to absorb, Tripp. There's actually a lot more, but perhaps we'll leave it there f..."

"So Howard is one of these people? Howard doesn't have a soul?"

"You could say that, yes, Howard is a Ziduga."

"Wow."

"Yeah, I know."

"I guess that explains why he did a lot of the things he did. He doesn't seem to care about anyone or anything. At least not in the same way that most people do."

"Yes, that is the root of it."

"What is that book about then? What does that have to do with this Ziduga people?"

"Yes, that's a very good question. There are some ancient texts that have been suppressed for thousands of years. Some of these texts, and I have never seen the texts myself, explain more of the history of this race, and perhaps other things that we are totally unaware of. No one knows for sure, except for those in possession of the texts. The Ziduga carry pieces of it and guard it very carefully."

"But wait, how is it that everyone doesn't know about this race? How could this be so hidden if they're all around us?"

"Another good question. People tend to see what they want to see, Tripp, and stay blind to what they don't want to see. The Ziduga are also very aggressive about keeping their secret hidden, to the point where threats are removed, and they have a very high success rate. I'm sharing this information with you Tripp, because I think you can help us. But having this information also puts your life in danger. You mustn't talk about this with anyone."

"Ok."

"If the Ziduga think they are threatened, the threat will be removed. It happens fairly frequently actually. But more than that, they also have an uncanny ability to operate in secret. Maybe you noticed that with Howard?"

"What's that?"

"That Howard could engage in all sorts of vile behavior and never seemed to get caught?"

Tripp thought of the incident with Mr. Tyler in the woods.

"Dr. Siderow was convinced that this race is involved in a mission on this earth, and there is not much that will stop them from trying to achieve that mission. I'm not sure I agree with that. I honestly don't know. But what is clear is that the Ziduga have operated throughout this world for millennia and have largely operated in secrecy. They have also managed to conduct their operations without getting caught for the most part."

This all struck Tripp as very surreal, and he suddenly had the sensation he was in one of his visions again.

"So now, you may be wondering why I came to you. The answer is, we would like your help."

The conversation became very real again. "I don't know how I can help. Like I said, I haven't had contact with Howard in a long time. And in fact, I really don't want to. There were some policemen who also asked for my help, but we said the same thing. What can I possibly do?"

"I think we can track Howard down. In fact, I have a pretty good idea of where he might be. I also think that he trusts you. In fact, you may be one of the only people in the world that he trusts. With your help, I think we can get to him. Tripp, you have to understand how important this is, and how important your involvement is. If nothing is done, Howard will continue destroying everyone and everything he comes into contact with. He may stop from time to time, but he will always resume again sooner or later." He paused then looked Tripp right in the eyes, "You know, without someone intervening, he will never stop doing what he's doing, and you may have the power to stop him."

Tripp took those words seriously, but he also had the sneaking suspicion that Peter O'Neill had other intentions. Not that he didn't honestly want to halt Howard's path of destruction if there was some way he could do that.

"Why do you care so much about this? And if there are so many of these Ziduga out there, what's so special about Howard?"

"You're asking all the right questions, Tripp. Dr. Siderow was convinced that there was a lot at stake here. In fact, not a lot, but everything. I'm pretty sure he lost his life because if his conviction that the Ziduga are starting to mobilize and something profoundly bad is going to happen. He didn't know what, and I don't either, but I see the progression happening now. And the worst part is, it's happening right in front of our eyes and almost no one can see it. That's the really frightening part. I have thought of trying to get the word out, but that's what Dr. Siderow finally decided to do before he died, and that's what cost him his life. We need to make the world aware, but in a way they will see and understand. Even if I tried to explain what's going on to people, they would most likely think I was crazy, and then I would have my food poisoned like Dr. Siderow. Nothing would be accomplished. No, we must be smarter than that. That's why I want to start a coalition, because there are others of us out there that know the truth, but perhaps don't want to acknowledge it, or feel it's safer to ignore it. There's strength in numbers, but building numbers takes time and it's very risky." He folded his hands almost as if he were about to pray, then grabbed the edge of the table.

"Tripp, I care about this because I don't

think I have a choice at this point. I think whatever is beginning to unfold could be the end of this world as we know it."

He smiled and chuckled. "That's an REM song. Funny."

"REM?"

"Oh yeah, you're too young. They were a rock group in the 80s. Anyway, that's why I care. And as far as Howard is concerned, our belief is that he is their leader."

"What?" Tripp's eyes went wide.

"Yes, again, we have no way to prove this, but our belief is that he is a descendent of Cain, which makes him the leader of the Zidug."

"You mean Cain in the Bible?"

"Yes, exactly."

Tripp was trying to get his head around everything he had just heard. He saw the sincerity and passion of Professor O'Neill, but Tripp wasn't sure he felt the same way. Perhaps he was just hesitant to get involved, or perhaps he didn't believe that any of this was actually true. He decided to probe a bit further to test it.

"I would think that if this race was going to impact the world in some way it would have done that by now, no? I mean, didn't you say they've been around since the beginning of the human race? Why is this happening now, after all this time?"

"I wonder the same thing myself. I do believe, however, that the answers to many questions, including that one, are in those texts that are guarded by the Ziduga. The texts themselves are called the Zidug. I asked you about the text that Howard carries because I believe he has a copy, or at least part of one. That's another reason it is so important that we reach Howard, and I don't know anyone else that he would listen to other than you. Dr. Siderow actually told me to try to find any connection to Howard that I could, and you were basically it." He leaned back in his chair and stroked his chin.

"I don't know how the copy ever got into the hands of Howard's parents, though I'm sure it's because of their lineage, albeit distant, to Cain. But regardless, the contents of that book could make a huge difference in the future of this world. I know it sounds crazy, but I firmly believe that. I also know that we are closer to that copy than to any other copy; in fact, I am not aware of any other copy. Many of them were most likely destroyed, and at the end of the day, that information could save countless lives." His face turned solemn. "Tripp, we have a responsibility here. Whether it's our destiny or just dumb luck, we have been placed in a unique position to possibly change the course of human history."

Tripp found himself moved by the gravity of Professor O'Neill's words, but he was still deeply skeptical. Suddenly it struck Tripp that if there was some evil force moving things in the world, then there should presumably be some force for good also working against it? He suggested this to the Professor.

He stood up and smiled. "Yes, Tripp you're absolutely right. I couldn't agree more. And I believe that at this moment in history, that force for good is us."

Tripp's mother arrived home as Peter O'Neill was getting ready to leave. She was a little troubled to find a strange man in her home without her present. Peter O'Neill introduced himself and explained that he thought she was home and would have waited for another time if he knew she wasn't.

"You have a remarkable son, Ms. Talbot. And he can play a very important role in our mission."

"Well, thank you, Peter, I would have to agree with you, but what mission are you referring to?"

"We believe that Tripp can be assistance in stopping a major catastrophe from happening. His special relationship with Howard is critical and I believe will be instrumental to our efforts. Tripp, do you mind if I have a word alone with your mother, please?"

Tripp obliged and retreated up the stairs while the two of them stepped out the front door and continued their conversation on the front lawn. Tripp was hoping he would be able to overhear them, but he couldn't catch what they were saying, even after opening the upstairs window.

After what seemed like an agonizingly long discussion Professor O'Neill left and Tripp's mother entered the house, clearly concerned, but resigned. She had agreed to allow Tripp to accompany Peter once she saw the travel plans, and as long as arrangements were made to minimize and make up any school missed. Tripp was shocked he was allowed to go at all.

CHAPTER 24.
RECKONING

Three days later it was agreed that Tripp would accompany Peter O'Neill and some others on a trip to Phoenix, which was the closest airport to where they believed Howard and his followers could be found. There was some speculation that they had left the United States and entered Mexico, but that theory had been put to rest when he had been identified near the border of Arizona and New Mexico several days before.

O'Neill had arranged for a car to meet Tripp at 6:30 am the next morning to take him to the airport for a 9:00 am flight. The rest of the group, including O'Neill, would already be in Arizona. Tripp would meet them once he arrived.

Tripp tried to go to bed early, but he had a lot of nervous energy that prevented him from sleeping. He didn't feel prepared for the trip, but he did feel compelled to help in any way he could. He was excited to be a part of this secret, yet seemingly world-changing mission, and he reveled in this sense of importance. His life meant something, and it felt good. It helped to keep the terror, that seemed to emerge at random moments, at bay.

He had a small bag packed and was lying in bed, staring at the ceiling as the minutes ticked away. The red numbers on his digital alarm clock showed it was already 11:48 pm. He wondered what Howard was doing at the moment in Arizona, a place he had never been before. He hadn't seen Howard in years. Did he look the same? Would he even recognize him? Time would tell. Tripp tried to imagine arriving at Howard's house......*and he slowly mounted the front steps. There was a staircase leading up to the front door, but the staircase didn't go high enough to reach it. He climbed to the top step and stretched as far as he could, barely reaching the door to knock on it. He waited, but there was no response. He banged on the door. No response. He tried again. No response. He was about to give up when it cracked open with a solitary hand extended through the crack. Tripp reached for it and it pulled him in. Inside, the room was square, dark and completely empty. Howard was seated on the floor in the middle of the room, and Tripp joined him. They sat facing each other and Howard began speaking, but Tripp wasn't paying attention to the words because he noticed he couldn't move. He was weighed down and the weight was so heavy he couldn't even lift his arms. He sat immobile, moving only his eyes to take in the room around him. Howard then stopped speaking and stood up. He produced the sacred book, wrapped in cloth, dirty and torn. "Tripp, the book has all the answers. The book.*

Read the book."

*He wanted to reach out for the book and take it from Howard, but no matter how hard he tried he couldn't move. Now even Tripp's eyelids felt heavy, and the weight shut them as well. Suddenly he felt like the weight was descending on him and the room and smothering his entire body. He laid down on the floor to get away from it, but it was overpowering. And then he went dark. Tripp couldn't tell how long he was in that state, but next awareness he had was of a jarring noise coming from the corner of the room. The room was pitch black so he couldn't identify the source, but he realized the suffocating weight was gone. The noise continued, ring, ring, ring...*Tripp opened his eyes and identified the ringing as his alarm clock. It was 5:45 am. He groaned, hit the snooze and rolled over.

Mustering his energy, he rolled out of bed and stumbled into the shower. He mechanically got dressed, still half asleep, and was stuffing his toothbrush and comb into his duffel bag when his mother came in to check on him. She had some breakfast ready for him downstairs, and by the time he finished eating and listening to her warnings and caveats, the phone rang. The car was out front waiting for him. It was 6:27 am.

The drive to the airport, the check-in and the flight itself were uneventful. Tripp slept, off-and-on, for most of the flight. Several hours later he was awakened by the captain's announcement that they were making their descent into Phoe-

nix International Airport. When he deboarded the
plane in Phoenix and made his way to the bag-
gage claim area there was a driver holding a card
with Tripp's name written on it waiting for him.
He didn't have any luggage checked in and the
driver escorted him straight to his parked car. He
informed Tripp that the drive was close to an hour
and a half. Tripp thought he might sleep some
more, but the novelty of the surroundings and
the bright, intense sunlight prevented that from
happening. They quickly left the tall buildings of
Phoenix behind them to cross the desolate, sun-
baked, yet beautiful desert landscape. Tripp had
never been in the desert before, and he found the
cacti and unique rock formations mesmerizing.

After a while, the novelty started to wear off,
and the terrain started to seem monolithic. There
was rock, sand and scrub brush as far as the eye
could see, with the occasional passing car on either side of the 4-lane highway slicing the desert
in half. In spite of the monotony, the drive passed
quickly and they arrived at the hotel, just off the
side of the highway, on the edge of a small town.

The hotel was small, but looked comfortable
and quaint from the outside. The driver pulled
up to the front entrance and opened the car door
for Tripp, letting him know that his party should
be waiting for him inside. Indeed, upon entering
the lobby he found Peter O'Neill sitting on the
couch waiting for him. He immediately jumped up
and extended his hand to greet him energetically,

"Welcome Tripp! Glad you made it. Hope the trip was smooth?"

"Yes, thank you. I slept for most of it."

"Well, nothing wrong with that. So, I already have your key for you. You're in the room next to mine." He handed Tripp the key for room 203.

"Are you tired, or hungry? Would you like to have some lunch?"

Actually, Tripp was neither. He wasn't quite sure what his state of mind was. "I think I'm all right for now."

"Why don't you get settled in your room and then meet us in the restaurant."
He pointed to the dimly lit grill at the end of the lobby.

Tripp agreed and went to his room to drop off his backpack. The room was basic, but sunny and welcoming. Out of his window he could see what appeared to be the main street in the town just around the corner from the hotel, a few blocks of retail shops extending out from the center, followed by increasingly sparse apartments and homes, then the endless expanse of desert. The horizon was punctuated by jagged mountains emerging though a settled haze. Leaving his bag on the bed, he made his way back downstairs to the grill. He immediately spotted Peter sitting with three others at a corner table in the back. Though surprises were commonplace in his life these days, he was still completely caught off guard when he recognized two of Peter's companions: Pastor Tom and Bubby.

On seeing Tripp walking toward their table Pastor Tom stood up to greet him. "So good to see you Tripp! Glad you could make it!"

"Tom?! How are you here? How do you know Professor O'Neill?"

"We'll get to all of that soon enough."

Bubby acknowledged him as well from her chair, and Tom introduced Will Mittford, whom Tripp didn't recognize.

"Please have a seat and join us Tripp," Peter motioned.

As Tripp sat in the empty chair between Bubby and Peter, he asked Bubby how she knew Pastor Tom as well.

"It's a small vorld, Tripp." She gave Tripp one of her rare smiles. "Sometimes zere are reasons bigger zan us zat vill make friends of unlikely companions."

Peter concurred, "Yes, Tripp we're all trying to accomplish the same thing here. That's essentially what brought us together. There are others as well, and I'm sure there are other groups of us that we're not aware of. But our numbers are relatively small."

William added, "There are risks inherent in what we're doing now. We don't want to be naïve about it. Those risks mean that those who are awake to the truth just keep it to themselves. We decided not to tell you about the others in the group until you got here because in this case, the less knowledge each of us has, the better."

"Yes, I understand. But, Pastor Tom, I've known you for years and I had no idea that you were involved in this. I mean, I wasn't really aware of how all this fit together until I met Professor O'Neill a few days ago."

"Just call me Peter, Tripp, we're all on a first name basis here."

"Ok, Peter."

"Tripp, do you remember when you asked me about that picture in my office some time ago, the one where I'm holding the fruit?"

Everyone at the table bristled at the mention of the fruit.

Peter clarified, "I haven't told him about the Tree yet, Tom."

"Ok, well, Tripp, That's a big part of this."

"I remember the photo, but what's so special about it?"

"I'm sure you remember the story of Adam and Eve from Sunday School?"

"Sure, I remember. And Peter told me about the Ziduga, from Cain."

"Right. So, there is the Tree of Knowledge of Good and Evil in that story, and God forbade Adam and Eve to eat from it. But they ate the fruit anyway."

Tripp nodded, and Tom continued.

"That tree exists. I mean, the original tree is most likely long gone, but there are descendants of that tree producing fruit all over the world now. The tree is the symbol of this people, the Ziduga, who want to destroy our world. History is unfolding in front of us, and the bottom line is this: God has a plan to remake this world, but this race, the Ziduga, are hell-bent on destroying it before that happens. And the time is close."

Tripp nodded that he more or less understood what Tom was saying, though he did have a lot of questions.

"Tripp," Peter continued, "we are going straight to the source to stop them."

"The source?"

"Yes, the source. There is a massive and growing community of Ziduga living out here in the desert. They are coming from all over the world and, as I told you, they are everywhere in our midst. In spite of the fact that they have no soul, they are masters at hiding that fact. Most people cannot tell that they are any different from you and me."

"Zat is vy ve cannot speak openly about zees. Like Peter said, zey are everyvere Tripp. And zey vill kill anyone who stands between zem and zer goal."

"But how do they plan to do it? I mean how do they plan to accomplish their mission of destroying everything?"

Tom took the question. "If you remember Tripp, the Tree gave Adam and Eve knowledge of Good and Evil. That's where it starts anyway. But over time, and now we're talking thousands of years, continued consumption of the fruit of that Tree eradicates the soul. No one knows where the soul is in the body, but consciousness, awareness, knowing good from evil, humans have it nonetheless. Eat from that Tree and the soul disappears."

"And zey have been vorshipping zat tree since ze beginning of time. Zey are soulless to ze core. It is irreversibly in zeir genes and zeir race as ze Ziduga."

"And," added Tom, "they continue to venerate the Tree and drink from it. In fact, they are growing thousands of them in the desert here."

Tripp thought for a moment, "But what happens to other people that eat or drink it?"

"Exactly the right question, Tripp. It begins the process in non-Ziduga too, and that is the key to their plan. The effects are gradual and probably imperceptible, but most definitely real. Ultimately, they plan to create a planet full of beings without souls."

Peter clarified, "We know of this community here, and that there are communities like them all over the world, growing massive quantities of this fruit. They have been at it and accumulating it for several years now. We believe the end game is to make Zid ubiquitous in the world's water supply."

"Zid?"

"We call ze fruit 'Zid' after ze race of ze Ziduga."

"I see. So you plan to stop this from happening."

They all nodded.

"But if this is going on all over the world, how can just the five of us do anything?"

"We can't Tripp," Will answered. "We have to believe that there are other groups like ours hopefully doing the same thing, but we don't know that. Our efforts to create a larger network haven't been successful. All we know at this point is that this site here in the desert is the main organizing point for the United States and possibly beyond, so that's where we'll start. We'll keep going until we can't go any further or until our task is done."

Tripp wasn't sure if it would work or not, but he trusted the group, and he was there to help. "How are we going to stop them here then?"

Will got visibly more animated at the question. "The fact is, the weapon the Ziduga plan to use to destroy this world is also their weakness. We want to take their weapon and us it against them, by destroying the source. We need to destroy the Trees wherever they grow. Without a constant supply of the fruit, it turns out their minds and bodies begin to shut down. Their bodies are different, but they still need it. They're like addicts."

Tom added, "Our ultimate mission can be nothing less than destroying every one of those trees on this planet. If even one survives, then we have failed. There can be no exceptions."

"That seems impossible. How can we even

be sure?"

"There's no question it will be challenging, Tripp, but we have no choice. Fortunately, we don't have to start with the end goal. We're going to start with this location here. It turns out that the Tree will grow in just about any environment, even the high desert, and there is a vast swath of land about sixty miles from here that is covered in them. It's bordering on an Indian reservation. They've been operating out of that location, pretty much unnoticed, for quite a while, probably years. And there are thousands of Ziduga who have now congregated there. That number is growing by the day."

"Yes," Tom added, "they are in the tens of thousands at this point. We have a contact, whom we know we can trust, who is a member of the county police force out there. He was first informed by the Native American community. They got concerned when the Ziduga population kept growing. He has done some investigating of the location and he informed us that there is an underground water source supplying those trees."

"Ve are going to poison ze trees to kill zem all. Zey vill not know until it is too late."

Tripp wondered, "But how can I help?"

"Well, Tripp, we are limited in numbers as you can see, so another pair of hands is always good." Tom hesitated before continuing. "This is also very risky. We know that if word got out of our plan, or if anyone from that community suspects us, they will not hesitate to stop us."

Will continued his thought, "And we understand that you have a somewhat special relationship with this Howard, who is their leader."

"Peter told me he's a descendant of Cain."

"Yes, it appears so. He is also in possession of one of their sacred texts. There is a belief among them that those texts only end up in the hands of direct descendants of Cain himself. We don't know if that's actually true, but that is the belief. Regardless, Howard is a leader of this community. We have that verified by someone who infiltrated the group."

Tripp was astonished at that thought, "You mean someone pretended to be one of the Ziduga and lived in that community?"

"Yes, for a time, but he was unmasked. The Ziduga can't be imitated for long. The contact was found out and disappeared weeks ago. We got a lot of intelligence on the community before that happened though."

"He vas vith zem almost three veeks, before zey caught him."

"Wow," was all Tripp could say. It still all seemed so surreal to him.

"So, Tripp," Will resumed, "if we are caught or even suspected of being a threat before our mission is accomplished, we will most certainly all be killed and this will all have been in vain."

"Unless Tripp," Tom leaned in and looked Tripp gravely at Tripp, "you are able to somehow convince Howard otherwise. He wouldn't listen to any of us, and he may not listen to you either if he thinks we're threatening them in any way, but it may be the only hope we have."

The table went silent for what seemed a long time.

"So," Peter addressed the four of them, "we are not going to waste any time. The longer we wait, the more risk there is of getting caught. Our plan is to go tonight. Tripp, you now know pretty much everything there is to know. We will leave once it's dark at 9:00 pm and will head straight to the water source access which our contact mapped out for us before he was caught. We have the chemicals necessary which should be more than sufficient to do the job. There is an entry point in the mountains about two hours from here...."

He noticed the waitress coming over to their table and paused to smile at her.

"Can I get you folks anything else today?"

"Why no, thank you Claire. I think we're ready for the check."

"Alrighty then. You got it!" And off she went.

"We will head there and conceal the car, then walk the rest of the way. It will take some time once we enter the tunnel to reach the water source. Probably another hour."

"As I can't valk all zat distance. I vill stay with ze car and vatch for people vile ze four of ju make ze journey."

Tripp nodded that he understood.

The waitress returned and placed the bill face down on the table. "You all come back again real soon now!" And was gone again.

Peter grabbed it and stood up. "I'll take care of this. It's 2:00 pm now. We all need to go to our rooms and try to rest or sleep if we can. It will be a long night. Do not answer the telephone and do not answer the door to your room no matter what. Don't speak with anyone. And I will see you all in the lobby at 9:00 pm sharp."

They all nodded in agreement and left in silence.

C HAPTER 25.
IN MOTION

Tripp walked into the lobby as he saw 8:55 pm on the clock behind the check-in desk. Everyone else was already there, though they weren't sitting together. Peter walked up to Tripp, greeted him cheerily, though Tripp could detect the heavy weight of their mission under the lighthearted façade, and beckoned him to leave with him.

Once they exited he took Tripp to the car parked on the side of the hotel and they waited as the rest of them came out one by one.

"We don't want to raise suspicion by all of us leaving as a group at this hour."

Once everyone was in the car Peter pulled out of the hotel parking lot.

Tripp was sitting in the back seat of the car with Bubby and Will as they left the small town in silence, and soon reentered the desert. It was a moonless night, with just the glow of the stars reflecting off the rolling waves of sand to light up the barren landscape. Tom was in the front passenger seat and turned to say something to the three of them that Tripp couldn't make out over the warm, dry wind blowing in through Peter's open window. Tripp figured he would tell them again if it was important. Apart from that, no one spoke a word for nearly the entire trip. Everyone was contemplating what was to come.

It was a straight shot on the same highway for nearly two hours before they turned off on a gravel road. They were heading straight for the mountains at this point which loomed large in front of them. Turning again they went down into a small valley amongst the hills and traveled another twenty minutes before coming to a stop on the side of an embankment. Peter slowly inched the car behind a massive rock outcropping until it was no longer visible from the road. Peter turned the car off and turned to look at the group, who were now all anxious to get out of the car.

"Are we all prepared for this? It's about a twenty-minute hike from here to the entrance. We can't drive any further, so we go the rest of the way on foot."

Tom and Will started to climb out of the car, followed by Bubby who stood outside the driver door while discussing something with Peter. Will got a backpack out of the trunk.

"I anticipate the whole journey will take about two or three hours, Belsa. If we are not back by four, then leave the area before sunrise."

Bubby acknowledged the instructions as she climbed in behind the wheel and lowered the window.

"Ju vill be back. Just make sure ve are successful."

Peter nodded and according to the dashboard clock at 11:38 pm the four of them were off.

Tripp looked up and saw more stars canvasing the sky than he had ever seen before. The terrain was dark, but now there was a crescent moon, low on the horizon and invisible behind the mountain, that gave them more than enough light to see their way along the path in front of them. It was clearly not travelled often, and several times they scrambled over large fallen rocks that blocked off the path. A bit further in, Tripp began to hear the faint sound of running water, though the source wasn't visible and the sound went in and out. They continued along the same winding path until they arrived at a hole in the side of the hill. Tripp didn't even realize there was a hole there until Tom and Peter started removing rocks and scrub that filled it in. Will and Tripp helped as well and when the opening was large enough for them to enter, Peter took a step in and beckoned for them to follow.

Inside the tunnel it was impossible to see anything. Will took two flashlights out of the backpack and took the lead, handing the other one to Peter. A bit further in the flashlight caught the shadows of an inscription roughly etched in the wall of the cave. Will stopped to inspect it and read it somberly to the group:

Creation awaits justice
Wrongly accused, wrongly punished

*Cain's descendants will remove the veil
And right the wrongs of history*

The group pondered the words but didn't acknowledge their meaning, at least not to one another. After a quiet moment, they turned and resolutely continued on the path.

They walked for some length of time, though time seemed to stop once they entered the tunnel, and nearly tripped over several large, plastic liquid drums stacked on the side by the wall.

"This is what they left for us," Peter said pointing at the five containers. "Just one of these would be enough to kill thousands of acres of any plant, but we can't leave anything to chance. Tripp, this may be too heavy for you to carry..."

"I can do it." Tripp heaved one of the large containers on his shoulder and nearly dropped it. It was much heavier than it looked. He lifted it up again, and once everyone was reasonably certain he was not going to fall over, they each grabbed a container as well.

"We'll have to come back for the last one." Peter also rested his on his shoulder and started off down the dark corridor. Carrying the containers meant Will and Peter were now relegated to holding the flashlights in their mouths to keep them focused on the path ahead. Will now took the lead.

The further down and into the bowels of the mountain they went, the narrower the tunnel became, and Tripp had to fight a growing sense of claustrophobia, which he kept to himself. Soon the sound of rushing water started to grow, and the flashlights illuminated trickles of water running, at times gushing, down the stone walls. Tripp was ahead of Tom, who was bringing up the rear, and both of them froze when they thought they heard a scrambling noise behind them. The others stopped as well. They listened intently but could hear nothing but the sound of rushing water, so they continued. Will warned them of a steep slope ahead as he started down, but the rock was wet and he slipped, sending the flashlight and his white plastic jug flying. The flashlight went out.

"Shit." The rest stood still.

"Will, you ok?"

"Yeah, I'm fine. I'm trying to find the flashlight. Stay where you are or you'll crack your head on that rock." He groped around ahead of him, trying to systematically sweep the ground for the light, while Peter assisted with light as much as he could without slipping himself.

"I found the jug!"

"Great. What about the flashlight?"

"Not yet." The wait seemed interminable. He had to go significantly further ahead than he expected to find the flashlight.

"Got it!" and the halo of light shone toward them some several feet down and thirty or forty feet ahead. As quickly as it brightened the corridor, they others heard it hit the ground and it went dark again.

"Will, what happened?" Tom asked from the rear. But there was no response.

"Will?!" Peter and Tripp yelled simultaneously, but they heard nothing but their echoes, muffled by the sound of moving water.

"I wonder if he hit his head. I'm going to try to get down this rock and find him."

"Be careful Peter. It's very slippery."

"No kidding." He turned to scramble down the rock backwards, but the rock was covered in water and slick. He immediately slid down the slope and off the side, falling a good six feet. He hit the ground off-balance, but managed to hold on to the jug and the flashlight.

"You ok Peter?"

"Yes, I'm fine. You guys wait there until I find Will."

Tripp and Tom stood in silence and waited. They couldn't hear anything at this point apart from the water, until Peter called out triumphantly from further down the path.

"Here's his backpack, just a few feet from the container. I don't see Will anywhere." He was scanning back and forth, now quite a distance ahead of Tripp and Tom, who continued to wait. "Where the hell is he?" He continued a bit further, until the glow of the flashlight grew faint.

"Peter," Tom yelled, "let's get the rest of us down there with you and then we'll help you look for him. Maybe he hit his head and passed out."

Peter came back to the drop-off. "The question is, how are we going to get back up there?"

"We'll figure that out when we get to it." Tom started to lower his container down to Peter who put it on the ground next to his and Will's, followed by Tripp's.

"Ok, Tripp. Your turn." He put the flashlight handle in his mouth and put his hands up to catch Tripp, who made the leap and landed.

"Tom, be careful." He put his hands up again, but Tom kneeled and tried to slide down. He managed to do it without injuring himself. They started searching for Will again, but quickly became frustrated and concerned.

"Where in the world could he have gone? There are no turnoffs on this corridor. He must be here somewhere. Here's another flashlight." Peter handed Tom the third flashlight from the backpack and continued to sweep with the light as Tripp and Tom brought up the rear with a second and third set of eyes and more light. But there was no sign of Will anywhere.

After retracing their steps three or four times to no avail, Tom finally suggested they continue on. "Maybe he's further down somehow. I don't know, but he's clearly not here. I think we need to finish what we came here for, then we can continue to look for him."

They reluctantly agreed to finish as quickly as possible and grabbed their containers again, leaving Will's where it was. Another hundred yards on they turned a bend, the three of them sticking as close together as possible. At this point the sound of rushing water muffled everything else and the floor had streams of water running downslope. The beams of light showed a gradually widening corridor at the end of which Peter identified a large a pool of water reflecting the faint beam.

"This is it. Let's do this as fast as possible."

They quickly made their way ahead to where the tunnel opened into a cavern and were all standing in a few inches of water. Tripp was soaked and exhausted. He felt like he had no more strength to lift the jug even if he wanted to. Peter immediately opened his container and started emptying the brown contents into the water which appeared to be moving swiftly.

"Tripp, give me yours."

Tripp complied and he repeated the process, doing the same a third time with Tom's.

"Ok, you two go grab the other two containers just to be safe and bring them here. He said to make sure to use all five containers."

Tom looked puzzled. "What are you going to do?"

"I'm going try to see if I can find Will anywhere around this cavern. There are several passages leading out and the water doesn't look too deep. I don't know where else to look. Just hurry back and I'll be here."

Tom took off, Tripp right behind him, the light guiding their way as they quickly retraced their steps to the original precipice where Will's container was still resting.

"Tripp, I'll hoist you up so you can go get the fifth one. Here's the flashlight. I'll wait here, just hurry. I don't know how long we've been in here, but it's been too long."

He offered his interlaced hands for Tripp to step a foot into and easily hoisted Tripp onto the ledge. Tripp landed on his hands and knees, which were now wet.

"Ok, I'll be back." Tripp was not sure he could lift that jug and carry it, but this was no time to fail. He would bring it back no matter what he had to do. He took the extended flashlight from Tom and started on his mission. He was glad he wasn't the one waiting by himself in the dark. Moving as quickly as he reasonably could, it seemed like the journey back took much longer than the one in. He finally saw the faint glow of night filling the entrance far ahead and spotted the fifth jug. He immediately grabbed it, and without wasting any time, started back yet again. He had to drop it and drag it along at times, even rest between segments, but he was proud of the fact that he wasn't going to let the team down. By this point he almost felt like he was in familiar territory, and he finally spotted the ledge in the distance.

"Tom! I got it!" But there was no response. "Tom!!!" He heard his echo reverberate down the tunnel. "Tom, are you there?"

Again, nothing but the sound of trickling

water. He wondered if he decided to head back to help Peter search for Will. Rather than wait, he slid his fifth container down the slope and tried to slide after it, with the flashlight still in one hand. He lost his grip on the container and it slid right off the side of the slope with a thud, then a splash.

"Oh no!" he shouted as he slid on the same path off the ledge, landing on his side with a heavy jolt and hitting his head on one of the containers. He laid still for a moment while he caught his breath, then sat up. His fear was founded: his container had split open with the fall and was lying empty several feet further down. He hoped that didn't doom the mission, but Peter did say that one container was more than enough. There was nothing he could do about it now, and the other container was still there. He stood up, grabbed it and resumed the walk, calling out for Tom as he went.

Eventually reaching the final bend again, he expected to hear voices and see the refracted glow of the other flashlight, but there was still nothing but rushing water and the illumination of his own light.

Maybe they found another exit? He thought to himself. Something was clearly not right. He called out both their names, but only water responded. He decided to quickly finish the job before there were any other mishaps and emptied the contents of the fourth jug into the pool of water in the cavern. He watched the current spinning in the center of the cave, but then it appeared to be rushing out the far end in one direction. He kept calling out their names and continued to get no reply.

He concluded that they had to have found another exit, but that he would immediately return the way they came. He would get out of there as quickly as he could, and they would surely be waiting for him at the car where they could all celebrate their mission accomplished. He threw the last empty container into the middle of the rock cathedral and turned to retrace his steps one final time. He couldn't get out of there fast enough.

Groping his way back through the passage he continued to call out for Tom and Will, but there was no response. Over and over he continued to assure himself that they would find their way back separately and all would be fine. He reached the precipice again and realized he had another problem, which was getting back up without any assistance.

Scanning the wall, he identified some crags in the corner where the walls met, and he hoped they would be secure enough to climb his way up. The first time he tried he slipped and fell back again. It took three more attempts, but he finally managed to claw his way back high enough to get a grip on the top and pull himself up. The rock was still wet and slippery and he almost slipped and fell back, but he managed to hold his position with a small outcropping under his foot. He was deeply relieved as he pulled himself up the rest of the way. He wanted to just lie and rest there for a bit, but knew he shouldn't waste any time and started running toward the entrance to the mountain. A few more minutes and he heaved a huge sigh of relief: he could see the dim glow of the moonlit entrance.

Emerging into dry warmth of the desert, he was ecstatic to be out of the confines of the cave. The partial moon was high enough in the sky now that he could clearly see his surroundings, including the path back to the car. He smiled to himself and started on the trail, excited to find the rest of the team at the car and for them to go celebrate. But when Tripp finally reached the car, he was out of breath and devastated. There was no activity and no one there. The driver-side door was open, but Bubby wasn't there, just the dome light and silence and greet him.

He checked out the surrounding area to see if he could spot anyone, but nothing. The desert was completely still, apart from occasional gusts of wind blowing through scrubgrass. He searched the car for the keys, but they weren't in the ignition or the glovebox. Not knowing what else to do, he got in behind the steering wheel and closed the door. He rolled down the window but locked all four doors for good measure. Yes, he would wait for them to make their way back. They would surely be back soon, especially Bubby who couldn't have gone very far to begin with.

The time was now 3:19 am on the car clock. Staring out the windshield and scanning for life in the desert in front of him he suddenly froze. He jumped up in the seat and looked around the car. It was faint, but undeniable. The smell of cigarette smoke was coming from somewhere, and for Tripp that only meant Howard.

He still couldn't detect any motion, so he stepped out of the car for a better view and gasped when he saw Howard seated on the ground with his back against the rear wheel. He exhaled a lung of smoke into the desert air and turned toward Tripp. Their eyes met briefly before he turned to crush the cigarette into the dirt beside him, then stood up. Apart from a bit more facial hair and looking a bit more muscled, he didn't seem to have changed much in the years since they'd last seen each other.

Tripp could only emit a faint, "Howard?"

He leaned back against the car.

"Your friends are gone Tripp."

Tripp took an involuntary step backward.

"We knew you were coming. We've been waiting for you."

"Huh?" Tripp was dumbfounded.

"One of your group was one of us. But it doesn't matter. Soon you'll all be."

As Tripp tried to decipher Howard's words, he started to feel more and more trapped.

"Who? How? No one in our group was a Ziduga. I'm sure of it."

"I'm sure you were. Tripp, you need to understand that we're saving the world, not destroying it. It's just a matter of perspective. There really isn't much you or anyone else can do about it. We have always existed in tension with one another, and the only way to end that tension is to remove one side of it. Only then will there be unity and peace."

"Unity and peace?! But the Ziduga are violent and destructive! How can a world full of destruction be peaceful?"

"Because there will no longer be an enemy, Tripp. There will be nothing left to fight. Our people were unfairly banished from human civilization thousands of years ago. We were left to fend for ourselves and against all odds we survived and thrived. Destiny is on our side; truth is on our side; the power is on our side. Everything on this earth has been evolving and leading to this final chapter. They thought they were banishing us, but really we were being set apart. This world was always meant to be ours, Tripp. The Tree was there for a reason. We are simply claiming what should have been under our dominion all along. And now, the world will have no choice but to either join us or die. It is quite simple."

"But Howard, you don't really believe that do you? If you forced the conversion of every last person on this planet to a Ziduga, there would be something else to tear everyone apart. That's not the answer."

"It's happening as we speak, Tripp. Your friends are in the midst of making that decision right now. And there are already far more of us throughout the world than you think."

It suddenly occurred to Tripp that he was probably next on the list, and that Howard brought others who were waiting nearby to take him back with them. Tripp suddenly panicked, and Howard must have noticed it.

"You don't need to fear for yourself, Tripp."

"Aren't you're going to force me to join you as well?"

"No, Tripp. You are free to go if you wish."

Tripp was confused and skeptical. "But I know all about you and the Ziduga. I know all about your plans to convert the world to your race. I know about the tree farms. I know it all. Don't you see me as a threat!?" Tripp realized he was yelling. He also hoped he hadn't just ruined his chances of getting away alive.

"No, Tripp."

He paused to light another cigarette, then added, "And I'm not concerned about you betraying us. The reason I've protected you all this time is because you are one of us."

He said it very matter-of-factly, and Tripp took another step backwards, bumping into the hood of the car. His mind and words raced. "Nooo-ooo, Howard, no. No, there's no way. I'm not a Ziduga. I would know it. I don't go around killing people. I, I..." He took a deep breath. "No, Howard. I can't be."

"You are." Howard paused again to let his statement settle in. "And deep down, you know it."

Tripp slumped to the ground, with his back against the car. He suddenly remembered how exhausted he was. He stared at the ground in front of him, motionless. His mind continued to race, and fight against itself. He tried to piece clues together. But it still didn't make any sense. It didn't add up. He couldn't be one of them. Sure, he wasn't perfect, but he certainly hadn't done the horrific things that Howard or the Ziduga had. Yet, at the same time, he couldn't seem to deny it either. His mind and body went numb.

Tripp finally returned and looked up. "So I can really go? You aren't here with others to take me back?"

Howard took some time before responding. "You'll be back Tripp. I guarantee it. And when you're ready, you'll know exactly where to go."

Tripp thought about these words. His fate was not written. He refused to believe that. And he certainly wasn't one of them. Howard was just playing games with him, probably to bring him into the Ziduga. Maybe this is how some people were brought in: they were tricked into believing their fate was sealed, and then through the community or the fruit, or whatever they were exposed to, slowly fulfilled their own prophecy. But not Tripp. He wasn't going to have any of it. He just had to get safely away and then he would tell the world. He couldn't let them win.

"Fair enough, Howard. I believe you. I know that you're right."

"No, you don't Tripp. You don't believe a word I'm saying. But the time will come when you will."

This was not the response Tripp expected, but he knew he had to stay strong and not doubt himself. That would be his undoing. He visibly stiffened, matching his appearance to his resolve, and pushed himself up off the ground.

"Ok." He wasn't going to argue this with Howard.

"We'll be waiting for you Tripp." And with those words, Howard turned and walked away, leaving nothing behind but his ominous words and a trail of smoke curling upwards into the night sky. No one else came out to take Tripp away, and soon, Howard was no longer visible behind the rolling desert hills.

Tripp continued watching to see if it was a trick, if Howard would suddenly return with a small army. But he didn't. Suddenly Tripp became aware of chirping desert birds and the dim streak of dawn peaking over the edge of the horizon.

He shook his head to force himself to wake up. "Ok, I need to figure out how to get out of here."

He spoke to himself to keep himself company. He really didn't know where he was other than the desert of Arizona. If there were keys he would have driven the car back, but he already knew the keys were gone. Feeling like he had no other choice, and that staying there any longer he would probably die in the coming desert sun, he decided to follow the dirt road out on foot. Perhaps he could hitch a ride if anyone passed this way. He didn't know how remote this place was. He gathered what little energy he had left and set out, constantly scanning the horizon for any sign of life.

As he began his trek he felt an odd mixture of terror and exhilaration. He was alive and free. He wasn't going to let his thoughts rest on Howard's words for another second. He had to believe, not just believe but know, that they were a lie. There was hope.

He had no idea how long it would take him to reach the road, so he just kept walking until he spotted a pick-up truck kicking up dust as it pierced the desert in the distance. Tripp almost cried. He wouldn't be able to flag it down, but at least he saw life. And his intuition was right: after making it to the road another car with an elderly couple stopped to pick him up. He was visibly disheveled, filthy and sleep-deprived, but he simply told them he got lost, and they didn't push further. Taking pity on him they drove him to the next town, and from there they helped him get a ride with a commercial truck driver in the direction of his hotel. He was back at the hotel late that morning.

C HAPTER 26. THE FINAL CHAPTER

Tripp's ticket home wasn't until the following day. He still held on to the hope that perhaps the rest of the group, or perhaps a couple of them, had managed to escape and would be at the hotel when he arrived or would return later that day. The front desk confirmed they had not returned to the hotel. They did not return to the hotel that afternoon or night either.

When he got to the hotel, he passed out on his bed almost immediately. He didn't have the energy to take off his dirty clothes, but he could only sleep for short intervals as he regularly woke with a start. He knew he was having disturbing dreams, but he could not clearly remember their content. He was, however, left with the vague impression and ominous feeling that they all had to do with Howard and the destruction of the world, and worse, that no one was doing anything about it.

It was this sense that in his dreams the world was not pushing back that troubled Tripp the most. After the third such experience, Tripp woke with the conviction that his work wasn't done. Intense daylight still pushed its way around the heavy drapes that were drawn in his room. He had to try to sleep some more, and he hoped that an answer would come to him. As of now he had no idea what else he could possibly do, especially by himself.

After another fitful couple of hours of sleep, Tripp decided to get up. It was now late afternoon. He knew what he had to do next, just not the best way to go about it.

He did the best he could to minimize his exposure in the town and to leave quietly. Eating some pizza for dinner at a local pizzeria, he returned to the hotel, then checked out the following morning. He interacted with no one apart from what was absolutely necessary. There were inquisitive glances from the locals, likely wondering why a boy who wasn't from there was wandering around by himself. He simply ignored them, trying to avoid people where he could. And when he finally fastened his seatbelt for the return flight, he breathed a huge sigh of relief and carried it the rest of the way home.

His mother was waiting for him when he walked off the plane at the airport. She gave him a hug, but didn't ask any questions about the trip specifically. She knew that he would share when he was ready. She did wonder where the others were and if they were returning separately. Tripp simply told her that he didn't know when they were coming back. Again, she left it at that.

For the following days, weeks and months, Tripp tried to go back to as much of a normal life as possible. But it was difficult to think about much else. He didn't know whether their trip accomplished anything. He had no way of knowing, and had to become comfortable with the possibility that he might never know. He did have one hint, however, that perhaps their mission was successful: Tripp didn't hear from Howard again. There weren't any more letters, and the distant reports of chaos seem to dissipate. An eerie and unsettled sense of calm seemed to descend and prevail in his world. He took that as a sign that they had accomplished their mission and that they had put an end to the chaos, at least for now. Perhaps they had been successful in destroying the orchard after all. In fact, with each passing day, Tripp grew increasingly hopeful that not only that chapter, but the whole book of the Ziduga had been written and completed. But the hope never had free rein. It was always tempered by a profound and ominous unease. He was always aware that he had another duty ahead of him, but the urgency seemed to wear off. He would wait until the right time.

Tripp never saw them the rest of the group again. Pastor Tom, Bubby, Will and Peter never returned. If one of them was a Ziduga, he did not know who. Surely, that was another lie of Howard's, meant to sow more confusion.

Pastor Tom's disappearance garnered the most attention in the town. His wife and children knew that he went on a trip to Arizona, but didn't know many details beyond that. Each member of the group traveled separately, and no connection was drawn between Tripp and the other members of the group. Tripp was tortured with not being able to tell Pastor Tom's wife what happened, but he could not. The family never resigned themselves to his disappearance and continued to hold out hope that someday he would return. Tripp knew that he couldn't provide her with any answers or any closure. Therefore, he kept it to himself.

Bubby's relatives were all distant, as far as Tripp knew, if she had any living relatives at all. People weren't even aware of her disappearance for quite some time. Tripp didn't know much about Will, Peter or their backgrounds and they weren't from the same town, so he didn't know how their circumstances resolved themselves.

And so, with time, Tripp found some semblance of an uneasy peace, though not closure.

EPILOGUE. SOME FINAL THOUGHTS

As I looked back through these events in my life, some still vivid, some less so, and read through my old journals, I still marvel at how these events unfolded. As a man of thirty-two, I don't go by Tripp anymore, a name I shed over a decade ago, but by my legal name Timothy. I suppose that means I grew up, though I have my doubts. In many ways I still feel like that scared little boy who played a modest part in trying to save the world.

Over the years I have gained a fair bit of perspective on what transpired, though I still find myself at a complete loss on so much of it. I still do not believe that I am a Ziduga, at least not by birth. It is true that my mind and body were altered to some degree when I unwittingly drank of the Tree myself. Witting or unwitting, intention appears to be of little import when it comes to these things. The juice Howard casually shared with me in the woods those many years ago, as we trekked through the colorful, falling autumn leaves to take a last look at the body of Mr. Tyler, was juice derived from the Tree of Knowledge, its ancestry going back millennia to the Garden itself. And as a result, unbeknownst to me, a process began that as far as I know cannot be turned back.

Fortunately, I drank very little of it, and my understanding is that the amount consumed, as well as the purity, seems to make a difference. Trees removed from the original over the vast expanse of centuries have far less potency and power. Nevertheless, as a result of that fateful drink, the war for my soul is always present. The visions I've experienced off and on throughout my life are a symptom of that cosmic wrestling match. And though I have never met one, I can only imagine what the half-Zids must struggle with day after day. I can see why they so often choose to end their lives.

Several years after the events of this book, my father left us and never returned. That was another loss that finally sank into my life after many years of searching and waiting and wondering. It took time to mourn that loss, as it did for my mother and sister as well. The fact that we do not know why he ultimately left for good, without a trace, made it all the more difficult. It also left a tattered question mark above the question of my origins. Though I have repeatedly put the issue of my ancestry to rest, the question still nags me from a dark corner of my mind. And if I did in fact come from the line of Ziduga, my father must have as well. There was a discussion I wanted to have with him but may never have the opportunity. I also watch my sister carefully. If I am Ziduga by birth, then she must be too. But she shows not the slightest indication of anything of the sort. And now, because this possibility planted by Howard raises more questions than it answers, I bury it yet again. There is nothing more powerful to the human psyche than a few carefully chosen words spoken to pierce our deepest insecurities.

As far as Howard is concerned, I have neither seen nor heard from him since that day in the Arizona desert some twenty years ago. I have many questions I want to ask him, but I have no way to contact him, nor do I want to. I try to let those questions go as well. At least for now.

From the time of that trip forward, an eerie calm continued to hang over the country, and even the world for that matter. I still don't trust it, even years later. I continue to tell myself that it's a sign that our mission was accomplished. Sometimes I fear that it may be a lull before the final battle.

And now, with awareness and maturity, I still find it miraculous that the world is not aware of this race of the Zids. But there is a code amongst them, including the half-Ziduga, that prevents that from happening, and this code has proven a more resilient bond than any. There is more to it than that, however, because any code, no matter how robust, will not prevent some from breaking it, particularly Zids who have no conscience to begin with. So, I explored this further. As a non-

Ziduga, you can never confront a Ziduga directly, because if they know you have identified them as a member of the race they will kill you without hesitating. Any inquiry has to be clandestine. I also discovered that the Ziduga not only won't divulge who they are, but they can't. It appears that the Voice will drive them straight over the edge of insanity before they could get that far, therefore it doesn't happen. I made the discovery myself by putting pieces of the puzzle together, but also because of my exposure via that fateful drink. I am not, however, the only one who has discovered the truth. Others, including of course Tom, Bubby, Will and Peter, who have come to the same realization, have chosen to keep the information to themselves usually out of fear for their lives. I have met others, though not many. They remain ever vigilant and rarely break their silence. Others who have revealed the secret invariably end up dead. Regrettably, I have seen that repeated too often. I'm not talking about Zids here, but humans. In my limited experience they seem to invariably meet their fate.

As for me, I too continue to experience something similar to the Zids, but not nearly to the point of madness or self-destruction. It just becomes extremely uncomfortable. In fact, writing this book has been an excruciating years-long process for me. At the risk of repeating myself (or perhaps because I'm trying to convince myself), I believe this is because of my exposure to the drink, and not because of my lineage.

But then, the question naturally arises, why in the world would I write this book? The answer is both complex and simple. Part of me feels as though it is what I was put on this earth to do. That is the easy part, and that is what became clear to me on that morning in Arizona as an adolescent. The Ziduga have been wreaking evil and destruction on our world for thousands of years, seemingly without anyone's full knowledge of what is actually at play. How many times have we heard about or seen something on the news so horrific we can't imagine how any human being could have engaged in such an act or series of acts? And the fact of the matter is, they couldn't. Only a Ziduga could have, and though there's no way I can prove this, I can pretty much guarantee that there is a Ziduga at the source of, or near, every single one of these horrific events. Awareness of the Ziduga will benefit humankind perhaps more than anything else possibly can. There may have been others in my situation before, perhaps who tried to do what I'm about to do, but didn't make it to the finish line. I have already accepted that I may meet the same fate. I am fully aware that once this book gets out, the Ziduga will first kill me, then go even deeper underground. I don't know if the belief that I am Ziduga by some of them, foremost Howard, will afford me any protection. I doubt it. But for me, the risk is worth taking.

Don't get me wrong. I also recognize that

knowledge is not a solution in and of itself. By the time you read this I will surely be gone. I discovered two years ago that I have cancer, and it was this discovery that inspired me to finally finish this book. I wanted to share what I have learned over my lifetime about this race, their history, and how there has been a hidden current woven into the fabric of human history. I have nothing to lose, as my days are most likely numbered anyway. The Ziduga can't take away that which I no longer possess. And if the cancer doesn't kill me first, I know they will. But that is not what made it so difficult to finally get this down on paper. I know it's the inner war in myself. I don't even know if anyone will believe a word I've written. All I can do is put it out there, each person must weigh it against their own experience. It can't be proven. It can't be disproven.

The bottom line is that this state of affairs in the world cannot persist unchallenged any longer. I have created a failsafe mechanism so that even if I die an untimely death, these words will be dispersed and read, to which you yourself are witness. We may be in a period of peace now, but I'm not convinced it will last. Surely the struggle will begin again, and throughout history the stakes in the battle between good and evil get progressively larger.

And if, by some stroke of luck, the current peace is permanent, if the battle has been won and the Ziduga have lost, then there is no harm in me sharing my story anyway. So, I've continued to fight against my own inner voices and to get my words down on paper.

And so, to those of who hold this book, I pray it has opened your eyes. Many will greet this message with deep skepticism, as I did even as a boy, and sometimes still do as an adult, even after everything I've experienced. There are days when it all seems like a distant dream. But there are others when it is far too real. Knowledge is power, and once the seed has been planted, it is difficult to deny the evidence, but not impossible. It is amazing how many of the world's mysteries begin to fall into place once truth is revealed. But perhaps even more amazing is how many choose to deny it anyway.

My ultimate hope is that the mask is removed and the pain, horror and destruction of the descendants of Cain are ended once and for all. Our world is a beautiful place, and the potential of the human race is limitless. I can only imagine what, absent the Ziduga, mankind might have accomplished over the course of these millennia. It is true, we have made a phenomenal amount of progress despite them, but it is now time to end this legacy and to fully unleash the power of the human spirit.

May God help us.

-Tim Talbot

ABOUT THE AUTHOR

David P Garland

David P Garland was born and raised in New England before setting out to explore the seven continents. A businessman and professor who now resides in New York City, he spent years studying philosophy in a village in the Swiss Alps and criss-crossing the halls of power in Washington, DC. David lives for balance, and works hard to create opportunity for those facing hardship via elected office and Project HOPE.

Made in the USA
Middletown, DE
18 December 2021

56520895R00149